# Sun City, 85373

## Savannah Hendricks

Grand Bayou Press

Library of Congress Control Number: 9798987543139

ISBN Paperback: 979-8-9875431-3-9

eBook ASIN : B0DBJZVM77

For Film and TV Rights – GrandBayouPress@protonmail.com

Editor: Krista Dapkey - www.kdproofreading.com

Line Editor: Gregory Filzen

Cover design by Savannah Hendricks

# CONTENTS

# Dear Readers

After twelve years as a medical social worker, I decided it was finally time to write a story where the main character held a job similar to mine.

My sweet English Labrador, Ransom, joined me on my driving adventure through Sun City when I began writing this story. While my job takes me into the retirement community often, it was summer and Ransom and I were getting cabin fever from being stuck inside, trying to avoid the heat. So a nice slow drive though Sun City was a fun adventure, along with a pup cup (which mostly ended up on his nose and the car seat). Because of my job, I've been able to go into over one hundred homes in Sun City, but a calming drive to soak it all back up was worth it. Especially since, at the time, I didn't know that Ransom would not be with me to celebrate the release of the finished book. This makes Sun City's architecture noted throughout the book extra special to me.

As you read, please note that Sharon's Angels is not a real company, however the emotions, both good and bad, that come with this line of social work are straight from what I and other social workers deal with daily. It's also why burnout and turnover rates are high in this field.

Yet, I wanted this fictional story to showcase the struggles and the joy that occur behind-the-scenes for those of us who work so tirelessly in this line of work. I'm grateful for those who show such kindness towards us. It really does make a difference. It's also why many of us have hung onto our jobs through it all.

This story mirrors the happiness, the fun, and the challenges we face every day.

I hope you enjoy your time in Sun City – remember if you ever come for an actual visit, bring your sunglasses, it's bright out here.

In memory of Ransom, who couldn't sniff out a piece of chicken if it was resting on his nose.

# CHAPTER 1

"What in the—" I push my flimsy, drugstore sunglasses up onto my head and blink hard.

It must be the scorching 118-degree heat causing the all-out senior-citizens-gone-wild party happening in front of me. There is one in hibiscus print swimwear floating on a bright-pink pool noodle. Another is in a rainbow-sprinkle-covered vanilla donut floaty while "Hammer Time" blasts through a speaker somewhere near the rectangular pool. A row of palm trees cast their shadows over the apartment complex's open courtyard. The stucco is an off-white color, and each arched top door is peachy-pink with gold numbers shining boldly in the center. It's as though I stepped back into 1970s Hollywood, and I'm waiting for a director to shout, "Cut!" through a vintage megaphone.

Instead, I hear, "Kelly!"

My Aunt Paula shoots her hand up in the air. She stands in front of an open grill; smoke wafting up around her like dry ice in a witch's cauldron. "Kelly!"

I roll my suitcase behind me; grateful the wheels keep it off the soaking wet concrete around the pool deck.

A woman steps in front of me. "*Bonjour*. You must be the niece Paula is always talking about. I'm Vivian, apartment 8." Vivian shows me apartment 8 with a glance of her eyes, looking up at the terrace that runs in a U-shape above us. I smell classic Avon Far Away perfume, and it reminds me of my childhood. Vivian is wearing a flowy floral robe and sandals with a slight heel. Her toes are bright pink and match the rims of her oversize sunglasses.

"Nice to meet you, Vivian." I ease my hand out and she takes it with a firm yet delicate grip, like that of her French accent.

Vivian leans in and doesn't let go of my hand. "We're charmed you can be here for your aunt. You look identical to your pictures on her walls, minus your short hair. I once went out and met with friends I made on the social media, and they were difficult to recognize, nothing close to their profile pictures. It was great fun, some of the nicest people I've met outside of Palms Place. And good news, not one of them was an axe murderer."

I touch the back of my head, where my hair stops at my neck. I give a crooked smile thinking about how Vivian's accent caused the word murderer to sound fascinating as *murdarar*. "I'm glad I could get away."

As I attempt to step closer to my aunt, a man with a worn T-shirt, the word *Marines* faded across it, gives me a nod as he moves in front of me. "I'm Herbert Carter, apartment 6. I didn't expect you to be so stalky." He reaches his hand out, and I shake it. "I don't like to be woken up by any type of late-night parties. I expect that even though you're a guest, you'll follow the rules we have at Palms Place."

"Turn down the music!" a male voice yells.

Before I can let him know I'm not a night owl, a woman comes up behind him.

"Don't worry, Herbert only *thinks* he runs this place." She leans around Herbert. "I'm Marie, the manager.

Apartment 1, under the stairs. Paula said your hair was short, but wow, that's short."

"Hammer Time" ends mid song.

I shake Marie's hand. "Nice to meet you."

"Herbert's right, her hair is very Meg Ryan." A lady in a one-piece orange swimsuit with a skirt bottom appears to my right. "Sorry, I'm Carol, Carol Noble, apartment 3." She reaches for my hand, although they're now tightly wrapped around my suitcase handle. Seeing this, Carol pats the top of my right shoulder. "We heard about the separation from your husband."

"You heard?" My voice cracks like I'm lying to my boss about taking those extra sticky notes home for personal use.

"Leave her alone." Aunt Paula's voice comes from behind the slowly gathering group. "She's here to spend time with me. I don't need y'all scaring her off."

I first see the top of Aunt Paula's shoulder-length milky-white-and-pepper-flecked hair, then the glimmer of Joy in her baby blue eyes. She does the same thing she has done since I was a kid, outstretched jazz hands. I allow her to wrap me up in them, and unlike all those childhood years, her shirt doesn't suffocate my face. Aunt Paula smells the same: rose water and figs. Only now there is the addition of the BBQ smoke that tickles my nose.

"You told them about Drew?" I whisper into her ear and then pull out of the hug.

"What did you do to your hair?" Aunt Paula holds me at arm's length.

"Cockroach incident at a client's house." I shiver just thinking about it. "So, you told them about my separation?"

"Do you think you're the only one whose spouse cheats?" Aunt Paula shakes her head.

"Of course not, but—"

A woman in a jumbo straw sun hat steps to my left. She takes a puff of her cigarette. "Rosa," she says with a spicy Spanish accent as the secondhand smoke comes wafting out. "Number two."

"Rosa, you must say *apartment*, otherwise it sounds like you are talking about making a BM." A thin and slightly bony, man of six foot plus appears behind Rosa. He's wearing an open Hawaiian button-down shirt and is a dead ringer for Magnum, P.I.—the original one, not the newbie. He clutches a can of something wrapped in a beer cozy. "George, a-part-ment 9. I've got a clear shot of your aunt's place and always keep an eye out for her. Safety-wise, of course." He winks.

I give a half smile, because I'm not sure if that's a good thing or creepy and glance at my aunt. Her eyebrows don't react, so I assume she's used to this sort of talk from George.

"And no, not *Sleepless in Seattle* Meg Ryan," George adds, eyeing my hair.

"Y'all know Kelly won't remember your names or apartment numbers. She's only here for the weekend. And her hair is *You've Got Mail* Meg Ryan." Aunt Paula's hand rubs the top of my shoulder. "Oh shoot, the burgers!"

Her flip-flops echo through the courtyard as she rushes back to the grill, lifts the lid as the flames dance around the circles of meat.

"I'm Fred!" a man in the pool calls. He has so much gray chest hair that it appears as though a cat has affixed itself to him. He's wedged himself into the donut pool floaty to the point he looks stuck. Fred lowers his sunglasses and gives a wave.

"Fred doesn't always remember his apartment number." Marie places a hand on my back, and thanks to my job, I'm not bothered by all the touching or the lack of personal space anyone is showing me. I'm used to strangers hugging me, patting my shoulder, reaching for my hand and giving it a squeeze. When I think about it, it sounds like I have some sort of perverted job.

"But I'm sure you know about his condition," Marie whispers. "With your line of work and all."

"It's a good thing he has all of you keeping an eye on him." I step forward and push my suitcase in front of me as Marie's hand remains on my back.

"Yes, I'm blessed to manage such a delightful place. The moment I saw Palms Place, I knew I was home. We might be in Sun City, but this place reminded me of the past. Like sunny Southern California, at that complex where Jack Tripper, Janet, and Chrissy lived."

"It does have a retro *Three's Company* look to it. But it seems more, *Melrose Place* to me." I gaze around. "I think those design shows call it California Spanish."

"We love it; I doubt any of us will ever move. The only reason we had a vacant apartment for your aunt was because"—Marie's eyes look down—"of the sudden death of Martha. And that reminds me, the only resident you have yet to meet is Beverly Hill, in apartment 4. She's resting. It's a bit too warm out for her right now. She loves fall. Everything with her is fall this or fall that."

"Beverly . . . Hills?" I lean on my suitcase's handle.

"No *s*. Just Hill. Beverly Hill. Her parents, Mr. and Mrs. Hill, had a sense of humor."

"I see." I fan the front of my shirt that has stuck to my skin from the heat. "It seems like Beverly and I should be friends. It's hot. I'm afraid I don't know how you do it."

"One grows accustomed to the summer temperatures. Hard to believe, I know." Marie sets her right hand on her waist.

I wipe the sweat off my forehead with my hand. "I'd love to put my suitcase away and possibly get some water."

"This will cool you off, hon!" Fred shouts from the edge of the pool as his hand comes lifting above the surface, bringing with it a spray of chlorinated water. His boastful laugh filters through the date palms around the pool, like fingers trying to block the blinding sunshine above.

"No need to rush off. Herbert will carry your luggage to your aunt's apartment." Marie motions for Herbert, who holds an empty plate in his hand by the grill. "Help yourself to anything in the cooler."

"You caught me just in time, Ms. Maria, otherwise that suitcase would have to wait until after my meal." Herbert approaches and snatches my suitcase before I can protest. "I got it." He snaps his fingers. "*Courage Under Fire.*"

I give him a questioning right eye.

"Meg Ryan in *Courage Under Fire*. That's what your hair looks like."

I touch my hair, trying to remember that movie, as the manager of Palms Place hovers by my side. "I'm sorry, but I thought your name was Marie?"

"It is, but nearly everyone thinks it's Maria. Not your aunt. She's good at remembering. I used to correct others, but I got tired of doing it."

Marie hurries off before I can respond, and Aunt Paula shoves an empty plate in my hand.

I'm expecting it to be a paper plate, so it takes me by surprise that it's heavy, causing me to almost drop it. Not wanting to be rude, I smile. I just want to get inside with the air-conditioning and sprawl out on the cold floor.

"You brought your swimsuit, right?" Aunt Paula slides a toasted sesame seed bun onto my plate, along with a patty covered in melted cheese.

"No, I don't own one . . . that fits anymore."

"With all those lakes and whatnot up in Flagstaff?" Carol asks over my shoulder.

"I'm more of a wade-up-to-my-knees type of person." I spot the cooler and move toward it.

Locating a bottle of water, I set my plate on one of the three glass patio tables around the pool. My hands are so sweaty it takes a few tries to open the bottle. The plastic crinkles as I suck half the water down and lower myself onto a chair.

The scratch of metal legs on the concrete causes me to turn to my right. All six feet plus of a man's name and apartment number I already forgot sits down in the chair next to me.

"You know, we aren't fancy here. You can swim in your clothes."

I peer over at him. *Magnum? No, that's not his name.*

He smiles. "George, a-part-ment 9. And I'm going to go with Charlize Theron. Just don't ask me to remember what movie."

My short hair has become an unexpected topic, and I run my hand through it. "I was thinking more Michelle Williams in *Manchester by the Sea*."

This seems to get a few nods of agreement, and I hope it ends the relentless discussion.

I pick up my burger with both hands. While most people wash their hands before they eat, or at least pull out some hand sanitizer, in my mind, it's pointless. When you deal with impoverished communities who can't afford cleaning supplies and go into care homes and hospitals, you realize that the stronger your immune system is, the better chance you have of surviving. Sort of like parents protecting their firstborn with bubble wrap, but by kiddo number three, they're dusting off the pacifier instead of sanitizing it for half an hour. And that the worst things, like C. diff, can't be killed with sanitizer. Being a germaphobe goes out the window after a year, even if it makes some cringe . *Adrian Monk would never have survived in my line of work.*

I take a bite, and the burger creates a flood of childhood memories of time spent with Aunt Paula and Uncle Andrew, her first husband. He passed away when I was twenty-eight. She remarried a man named Steve, who I never really knew too well. It was upon our recent monthly phone call I learned not only had Steve passed away, but that my aunt had moved out of the house. I have countless memories of my visits to her home in Sun City. Thankfully, the house had not sold yet. The summer housing market in Sun City was as slow as a lizard sunbathing on a rock.

Vivian pulls out a chair in front of me. "We're so glad you could come spend time with Paula. We know you've been dealing with your own plate of debacles."

I press my lips together, embarrassed.

"Not to mention your aunt dealing with the sadness she's hiding underneath an overabundance of cheer and a giving attitude."

"It's all her years as a teacher." I glance over at Aunt Paula serving up everyone's plates. "Hopefully, as long as I don't die from heatstroke, she and I can have some self-care time."

"Two days isn't too long." George tosses a salty chip into his mouth.

"Does everyone usually spend time outside? When it's *this* hot?" I take another bite of my burger, knowing full well that it and the cheese will stay warm no matter how long I take to finish it.

"When you get to be our age, you realize the importance of living life to its fullest, even if that means being uncomfortable," Marie says. "There are many studies about loneliness and its association with increased risks of anxiety, depression, heart disease, stroke, and dementia, resulting in premature death. This is how we combat it, by spending time together."

"She's a walking webpage, isn't she?" George grabs another chip. "We would go stir-crazy if we stay inside for weeks, summer cabin fever. We do what we have to, even if it means shoving ice cubes down our under britches. We have FNF every week. It's something we look forward to. Some of us are retired, some of us still work or volunteer. It's just a good way to check in, stay up on the happenings."

"FNF?" I inquire, covering my mouth as I continue chewing.

"Friday Night Fun." George has both hands wrapped around his burger, causing the bun to nearly disappear. "Depending on the weather. If it's summer, we're in the pool; spring or fall, you'll find us playing cards, board games, tending to the plants, dancing, or watching movies."

"You meet up in someone's apartment for a movie?" I ask.

"No, we hang a sheet off the terrace and pull out a projector." Vivian smiles as though she looks forward to movies the most.

"We always barbecue," George mentions.

"What if it rains?" I inquire.

"If," Carol states, standing over my shoulder, "it rains, it passes quickly, especially during a monsoon. It's the dust storms that seem to stick around. Have we ever missed a FNF?"

George and Vivian lock their eyes, questioning, and they shake their heads.

"Hey, Maria?" George beckons. "Have we ever missed an FNF because of the weather?"

I want to correct George. *Marie.*

But she responds anyway. "We did one time, it was 122. I think it was three years ago. I remember because my granddaughters, my son Aaron's kids"—Marie makes eye contact with me as she walks closer—"wanted to see if we could bake cookies on the sidewalk. And wouldn't you know, you can. A little flat but tasted yummy."

Aunt Paula serves up the last burger and finally has one on her own plate, and heads toward our table. "We're glad you could join us for this FNF. Even if it's a bit too hot for a Flag person." Aunt Paula winks at me.

Then, behind us, a man is jogging towards the pool.

"Cannonball!" he shouts, attempting to leap into the pool but ends up doing more of a belly flop.

"Fred!" the residents of Palms Place shout as a tidal wave of chlorinated water crests and splashes onto those of us closest to the pool. Meaning mostly me. I've only been at

Palms Place for twenty minutes and have already gotten soaked twice.

When I open my eyes, water drips down my forehead, and most of what remains of my burger in my hand is sopping wet.

"I'll fire the grill back up," Aunt Paula calls out as she springs up from the chair she'd only sat in for half a second.

I set my soggy burger on the plate. *It's going to be an interesting weekend.* But I smile, because it's the escape I desperately need from my life back in Flagstaff, even if I'll never remember all the residents' names.

# CHAPTER 2

I can't help but stare at Aunt Paula's scar. It runs from her elbow, stopping about two inches from her wrist, on the outside of her right arm. While it's a reminder of how strong she is, it's also a reminder that I've always had a chip on my shoulder over her second husband, Steve, leaving her alone to fend for herself while he was on a golf trip. The burglar took a knife to her after he tried his best to steal everything she owned. It's also why I'm happy she's surrounded by what appears to be a good community of residents at Palms Place.

"Why didn't you tell me about Steve passing until well after the funeral?" I ask.

"Oh, honey, I know how busy you are with your job and your husband." Aunt Paula sets her glass of iced tea on a coaster on the end table in the living room. "And you weren't close to Steve like you were with Andrew."

"I'm still upset you didn't bother to tell me about any of it until after the fact."

"Kelly, he passed away. There was nothing to bother you with. I wasn't going to let you drive two hours to give me a hug. What would you have done? Help me stare at a fancy rectangular box lowering into the ground and pack up a few boxes? Steve had already set up his burial needs; he was a man of few things. And I know how hard it is for you to catch up at work once you fall behind. Plus, the funeral was on a Wednesday."

"The point of you telling me is so I could be there for *you*."

Aunt Paula leans forward in her recliner and reaches for my hand. I give it to her as though she's going to read my palm. As a child, she'd take my hand and sneak me those strawberry candies, the kind in the crinkly wrapper with the hard shell that had the goop inside.

"What about me being there for you, Kelly?" She squeezes my hand.

"You have always been there for me. Any time I need you, you're only a phone call away."

"At least you call me. Now, do you want to talk about it, or are we going to continue to act like all is well?"

"About Drew? Or about his affair?" I choke out the words, still too raw to say aloud. "I can't believe you told strangers about it. It's embarrassing and none of their business."

"First, they're not strangers to me, and second, why would you be embarrassed?"

"He cheated on me because of something I did or didn't do."

"Blaming yourself is the most self-flagellating reason I've ever heard. In fact, it's entirely ridiculous, and now I don't want to talk about it."

"Fine."

"Well, I guess then we're even." She sits back in her chair.

The room is silent too long for my liking, so I break first.

"How long did it take you to learn everyone's name here?" The lump forms in the back of my throat that feels like a peach pit because Drew's affair was moved back into the foreground of my brain again.

Aunt Paula side-eyes me. She knows I'm a professional at redirecting conversations. A skill I've perfected over the years as a social worker. Strangers willingly tell me their deepest thoughts, life regrets, and spontaneously show me their unidentified sores developing under skin folds. I shiver at the thought. I don't even want to look at anything on me that's unidentified.

"I tried to create a rhyme to go with their apartment number, but it's not foolproof. I still forget a few names. Maybe I'm just too old to retain things like I used to."

"Aunt Paula, you're seventy-three. That's not old. I can tell you, with all the clients I work with, it's just a number. Just this week I assessed an eighty-nine-year-old woman who got off the couch faster than me." I slap the tops of my legs and snicker at the thought.

Aunt Paula cups her iced tea as the fan overhead helps push the conditioned air around. "Work is going well, or more of the same?"

"My caseload remains an overwhelming, out-of-control mess. But at least I can work from home now instead of driving into the office only to turn around and drive back out to meetings. They hired four new employees, but only two of them have stuck around. We're feeling like nothing we do matters anymore, just pushing paper around. I would've stayed longer than the weekend, but you know how hard it is for me to get away from work."

"I know, honey."

"Management sent out a reminder email for us to use our annual PTO before the end of the year. They claim vacations prevent burnout, but then our cases go unmanaged, and we end up coming back to a bigger nightmare than before we left."

"It sounds like a hamster wheel."

I nod and look around at the familiar furniture in the unfamiliar apartment. "Why didn't you tell me about putting your house up for sale?" The emotion I hold so deeply for her house surprises me. I didn't grow up in the house, just visited, but there was such peace and familiarity there, like attending your local church. It felt like I was losing the last of my childhood I so desperately needed.

"Because it's my house," Aunt Paula snaps.

My breath catches in my lungs. I don't expect this from her. She's never scolded or yelled at me, even when I left a crayon in my pocket that made it into her dryer and ruined an entire load of clothes. It's not that I don't deal with grumpy, upset people, but it truly hurts when it comes from family.

"I'm sorry, Kelly. I don't want to let it go. I have lived in that house since 1983. But with Steve gone, I knew instantly I couldn't manage it anymore. And running the air conditioning on one pension and social security check instead of two . . ."

Part of me understands where she is coming from. But it doesn't lessen the sting of her move to Palms Place. Her fragrance is in the air, and familiar photos are on the wall. But it's not the same. The carpet is different. It's a tan Berber not the ugly brown shag; and there is no backyard where I can smell the orange blossoms in the spring.

"We can stop by the old house tomorrow morning." Aunt Paula sighs.

A brief flicker of a flame that I thought was all but extinguished dances in my soul. "Thank you." I stand and kiss her on the cheek.

In the poorly lit apartment, her features are softened by the glow of the antique lamp with its mid-century scalloped-edged Capiz shell lampshade, allowing me, for a few seconds, to pause and notice how much she looks like my mom. Maybe that's why I feel extra close to her. Spending time with her always felt like I was spending time with Mom, even though cancer took her from me when I was nine.

I notice my purse is buzzing, and I shuffle, undecided, in my steps forward and then back. I dig through my purse and remove my work phone.

"Sorry, I must have forgotten to turn it off." I hold it up to show Aunt Paula.

"You brought your work with you?"

"Yes, you know how the I-17 can be on the weekends, especially in the summer. I didn't want to be stranded heading back home without the option to log in on Monday morning."

"Don't you dare be checking those voicemails," Aunt Paula warns me in that teacher tone she has perfected.

I notice five missed calls, four from the same number and one voicemail. "I have one message. I need to check it just to make sure it's not an emergency. I don't want to dive back into work on Monday with it hanging over my head."

"If it's an emergency, they can call 911." Aunt Paula stands from her recliner. "I'm not sharing my eatable cookie dough with you if you check it."

I freeze and grip the phone in my hand. Her eatable cookie dough is close to heaven on a spoon. In fact, I wouldn't be surprised if they offered it at the Pearly Gates. I know I don't need to check my message, but I also know that the clients we serve expect us to work twenty-four seven, seven days a week. Not that they bother to even say thank you. I scold my negative thoughts, running rampant with anger. I must find the positives, because otherwise I'll end up at the bottom of a dark rabbit hole again.

"I recollect"—Aunt Paula sets her hand on my shoulder—"that all my years as a teacher has a lot in common with your profession." She moves into the kitchen, but my skin is still warm from where she had her hand. "Angry parents, stressed-out kids, frantic school staff, and not enough of anything to go around."

I realize I'm holding my breath, and I let it go, setting my phone on the kitchen table next to my purse.

"You're only here for a day and a half. Try your best to forget about everything that's sitting heavily on those shoulders of yours." She grabs two small glass bowls from the cupboard. "I promise you, everything will be waiting for you on Monday."

Before I can respond that, of course, she's correct, there's a knock at the front door. I check my fitness watch. It's well after nine. "Expecting anyone?" I step to the door.

"Around here, seems as though someone is always stopping by." She removes the lid from the plastic container that she pulled from the refrigerator. "Go on, let's see who's behind door number one."

"Hi . . ." I say to the tall man standing in front of me as the heat from outside smacks me like a towel from the dryer.

"Apartment 9, George." His beer cozy is still glued to his right hand.

*Magnum.* "Yes, right?" I hold on to the doorknob while he tries to peer around me into the apartment.

"I just wanted to make sure you ladies didn't need anything. Including my company."

"Why, how kind of you, George, but I think us ladies can manage," Aunt Paula says from the other side of the kitchen's peninsula as she scoops the silky cookie dough into one of the two bowls. "Would you like to join us for dessert?"

George raises his head, and shifts his eyes toward the counter. "No thank you, not a fan of sweet things, even if it is cookie dough."

Aunt Paula puts the spoon into the container and comes around the counter and into the living room. "I'm envious of your outstanding eyesight. You can see that from there?"

"Yes." George laughs. "LASIK surgery. Best money spent." He glances behind him, steps inside, and closes the door. "Besides gracing you fine ladies with my exuberant company, I had a specific reason for stopping by."

Aunt Paula returns to the kitchen's peninsula.

"It's about Maria's son. The one coming tomorrow." George makes himself at home and plops onto the couch.

"Marie?" I say.

"Ah, yes, Mari-e. See, her son is without a decent place to live and so he's helping out his mom by managing this place while she's on her cruise vacation. Normally he only visits because he resides close by, but this time he's staying the entire month."

"And the issue?" I ask.

"He's a cop, the kind with a dog—a large cop-dog, K-9—and I'm slightly concerned."

"What for, George? We love his K-9. Are you hiding drugs in your apartment?" Aunt Paula asks.

"Does my cholesterol medication count?" He narrows his eyebrows. "All joking aside, our concern is that he might get into a disagreement with Herbert again. As you know, Herbert is sort of the rule police for Palms Place.

And what about Fred? He wasn't as bad before. Can a cop take away someone showing signs of dementia?"

"I don't know. Maybe Kelly can shed some light on the dementia thing?" Aunt Paula crosses her arms over her chest.

"Unless Fred wanders off or has some sort of disruptive or resistive behavior, a cop can't do anything. They can call Adult Protective Services, but even at that, there must be neglect or abuse. If Fred is orientated and isn't hurt, then there is not much anyone can do."

"That's good to know." George slurps from his beer can and rests his other hand on his knee.

"It's getting late," Aunt Paula states. "And my niece is trying to enjoy her weekend and *not* think about her job."

George glances around the room. "Right, yes." He stands. "You ladies have a delightful night."

I follow behind George as he makes his way to the door and pulls it open. It feels like he's opening the oven, and a reminder of why I live up north.

"George, what's the big deal with him bringing his police dog?" I ask, trying to hide the excitement in my voice. I love and respect service dogs.

"Palms Place has a strict no pet policy. Except for service animals. But it's sort of an ongoing argument between Herbert and Maria, because he feels an animal is an animal, service or not."

"Marie," I mumble, but George doesn't hear me in his alcohol fog.

"Night, ladies, thanks for the chat." He stumbles over the door's threshold, and I close the door quickly, hoping to escape the relentless heat causing my body to sweat in seconds.

I lock the door and look back into the kitchen at Aunt Paula. "His gait. Does he always shuffle his feet?"

"Please don't social-worker-talk to me. Gait? You mean walking?" Aunt Paula shoves the container into the refrigerator and carries the bowls toward me, meeting me in the middle of the living room.

"Yes, walking. Does he always drink? I mean, is it normal behavior for him to drink so much that it affects his walking?" I take the glass dish and make my way to the familiar couch.

"He got hurt in an accident at work, messed up his leg from what he told me. I don't think it has to do with alcohol."

The spoon, with creamy and sweet goodness, hits my tongue, and my eyes flutter with delight. But as I go for a second bite, there is another knock at the door. "Seriously-?"

"I'll get it." Aunt Paula takes her bowl with her and flings the door open, causing her silky gown to flutter in the movement. "Herbert."

I push myself further back onto the couch so I can see around my aunt.

"Good evening, Ms. Paula, and Ms. . . . my, give me a second. Ah, yes, Ms. Kelly." Herbert leans around my aunt. "I wanted to provide a quick reminder about the importance of the Palms Place rules, even with guests. I know Ms. Maria is already in the vacation mindset and probably didn't check with you about the tolerance for commotion after ten o'clock." Herbert holds his hands behind his back, his posture straight as a metal rod.

"I don't think that'll be a problem, Herbert. Unless . . ." Aunt Paula turns to me. "Kel, did you bring the fireworks I asked for?"

I pause, the spoon of dough midway to my mouth. "No?"

"What about the conga drum?"

"No." I shake my head in slow motion.

"Well, Herbert, then I think we're good." Aunt Paula beams a smile and begins to close the door. "Good night, Herbert. Sleep tight."

He still has a confused look on his face when Aunt Paula closes the door all the way. She spins around, her robe flying out behind her like a cape. "Let's watch an old movie, your pick."

I set my bowl on the coffee table and approach the entertainment center. Sitting on my heels, I dig through the DVD collection. Doing this brings me back to Aunt Paula's house and the countless memories it holds. It's where I go in my mind when work is overwhelming and I need to forget everything going on around me. Where I can find hope and happiness. Where my heart is light and full of love. A place where my husband didn't mess up our life together.

# CHAPTER 3

With every turn Aunt Paula makes through the neighborhood, excitement flutters in my heart. As she pulls into the driveway, I notice the Mansard roof has a few missing terracotta tiles, probably lost in one of the many monsoons over the years.

"How long has it been since you visited?" She keeps the Jeep idling and the air conditioner on high.

The sunshine continues to radiate through the passenger window and the skin on my right arm already feels like it's burning. "I think two years, I was here for you and Steve's 5 year wedding anniversary party."

I push open the passenger door and squint behind my sunglasses. The sunshine glares back at me off the house's white paint. The arched black gate is closed, but I can hear the trickle of the waterfall feature in the enclosed courtyard.

She slips a key into the lock and gives it a solid wiggle before it swings open, and we make our way into the courtyard. Nearly everything I remember being lushly green is now flopping over, displaying yellowish tinges with mixes of dead brown.

"The real estate agent is going to have a fit seeing these plants dying. I told her don't add anything during the summer, but she didn't want to listen. Newbie to the valley, she'll learn soon enough."

As Aunt Paula unlocks the right side of the front double doors, the memories release through a history of scents, hitting me in the heart, and I blink to prevent tears from instantly forming.

*Gosh, I miss how simple life was back then.*

A few steps inside, the white wrought iron flower pattern greets me, and I can see the kitchen beyond with light coming through the window over the sink. The living room wall to my right still holds the original full-length mirrors that allow the room to appear three times bigger than it really is. I move past the empty sunken living room and follow my aunt into the kitchen. The 1973 stove is still stuck in the wall, and instantly my mouth waters thinking of all the desserts I've helped bake, especially the prickly pear lemon bars.

"Why am I emotional?" I suck in a breath, realizing I've said it aloud.

"Because you have a lot on your plate." She tosses the keys onto the yellow Formica kitchen counter, and they echo throughout the empty home. "And you never give yourself a break."

I make my way into the family room and notice the wood paneling. Not that I forgot it was always there, but without the furniture, it really stands out. While I'm aware nearly everyone on earth now despises wood paneling, I love it. I've always loved it. Maybe because it reminds me of a house filled with love.

The fireplace has a fresh coat of moonlight-white paint on it, and the rest of the walls are a soft white dove. "Did you paint?"

"Everything but the wood paneling, it gives it a clean look. The realtor argued about that, but I stood my ground. The new owner can paint over it. There are bigger issues, such as stove knobs that don't work anymore. I had to use needle-nose pliers to turn it on and off, plus the dishwasher leaks. Too much stuff for me to manage, and whoever buys it will end up flipping it anyway, so I didn't want to bother with updates." She looks out the extra-wide slider into the backyard.

I step closer and join her. The water in the pool glistens. And it's then I realize the air-conditioning is barely keeping the place at a decent temperature. My tank top sticks to my back. "It's a little warm in here. Is that how it should be?"

"Keeping it cool was costing me a fortune. It's set at 85 just to prevent any potential buyers from catching on fire." Aunt Paula chuckles.

I wander off down the hall, and pause at the first spare bedroom, with the cherry-red carpet. My uncle Andrew was always deeply focused on his latest model cars and airplanes, and when I close my eyes, I can see him sitting in the room at the workbench.

Moving further down the hall, I pass by the other spare room. The one I once referred to as "my" bedroom because, as a child, I spent the night often. Now, the swirly royal-blue carpet looks like it needs a good scrub. My eyes pinch close as memories flood my mind and tears well up in my eyes. I want so badly to go back to that time. A time before I grew up and turned into an adult.

Aunt Paula comes up behind me, and together, we continue to the main bedroom at the end of the hall. The French doors are open, and we can see the pool out the three massive windows on the south wall. It's so bright I squint, and sweat forms across my forehead.

"I love . . . *loved* this house to the depths of my soul." I swallow the lump in my throat and try to keep it from getting thicker.

My legs weaken, and it takes determination to keep standing upright. I stumble forward, grabbing hold of Aunt Paula's shoulder. I gasp and place my hands on my knees as nausea rolls through me. *Is it anxiety or the heat?* I've been in many homes without air-conditioning, so maybe I'm dehydrated. The room grows hotter and hotter. Panic washes over me as I get goose bumps on my arms even though I'm sweating. Why is this happening? It's not even my house.

"It's going to be okay," Aunt Paula says as we move through to the bathroom and out the small door that leads into the backyard.

It grows hotter. The sun is so intense it hurts my skin. But my hand is wrapped tight around Aunt Paula as we move closer to the pool. A few more steps, and I feel cool-ness at my feet.

"There you go," Aunt Paula says.

I look down and see we're standing on the first of two steps that lead into the kidney-shaped pool. My flip-flops are still on my feet and the water is up to my ankles. Aunt Paula has taken off her expensive orthopedic sandals and set them on the pool deck. My flip-flops are cheapies from the grocery store, so being washed in chlorine doesn't wor-ry me.

She squeezes my hand. "It's going to be alright, honey." She glances over at me, then back at the house.

I shouldn't be so emotional about a house that isn't mine. But when I think about my marriage to Drew and my career, my breathing turns heavy again as the pressure in my chest returns full force. "This house is my happy place, my safe memory holder. It feels like you're taking away the only thing I have that doesn't have complications and worry attached to it."

"You haven't been here in a while." She steps further into the pool, the water reaching the hem of her jean capris.

"That's what I don't understand."

"There is a reason why you're upset about the house. You need to dig under all those layers you have built up to discover why."

"It's not that easy."

"It can be."

"Maybe for you. You're carrying on as though this home is a dead houseplant that needs to be taken to the trash. You built a life here. It's full of memories."

I hear her take a long breath. "Memories that remind you that the people you love are dead and you're alone? You can't fix death. You can only fix what's alive."

"And I can't fix the fact that Drew cheated on me and broke my heart like a baseball bat to a lightbulb."

We're both breathing heavily, and the sound echoes around us.

"I doubt you have sunscreen on." Aunt Paula turns and steps out of the pool and back into her sandals. "Let's get out of here."

Instinctively, I stomp my right foot under the water, causing ripples. I don't want to leave. I want to bake another batch of prickly pear lemon bars in the oven and roll out another eatable cookie dough on the counter. I want to sit on the patio late at night listening to the breeze blowing through the velvet mesquite and smell the scent of blooming orange blossoms.

I'm still standing in the pool when I hear my name being called. My aunt waves me in her direction. And like a sulking teenager, I huff, coming out of the pool, my flip-flops squishing out water as I cross the patio.

"I'll meet you in the Jeep." She holds out the single house key on the ring. "Why don't you say goodbye to this place?"

"What about you?"

She heads toward the front door and pauses. Without turning around, she says, "I already said goodbye."

I stare at the key in my hand as I hear the front door open and then close. Although the house is empty, it feels full of life. It's alive with memories. I can still see where the furniture once sat and smell the tangy sweetness of the prickly pear lemon bars. There is the sound of *Salute Your Shorts* on TV in the background. Squeezing the key in my palm, I start crying. Which turns into bawling like a baby, then into an ugly sob. But I can't stop, as I release what feels like years of bottled-up emotions. I'm crying about my marriage, my job, and the memories I hold of my wonderful times in Aunt Paula's house. Somehow, reliving the memories of my childhood causes me to realize how unhappy I have been the last few years. How I've only focused on getting by and not actually living. How I've allowed work to encase my life. And now, how naïve I was to think I'd always be able to come here when I *made* time. I'd made excuses. Was I no different from Drew making excuses for his infidelity?

This realization causes me to choke up, and I swallow hard. I can't take back the years I missed. I can't smile at memories that were never made. But I don't know how to fix it, to change my path, to make up for it. And as I glance around, it's as though the wood paneling is laughing at me, closing in. Reminding me I'm losing time, not gaining it.

Instead of taking everything in one last time and having a proper goodbye, I do what I do best—I ignore it. I wipe the tears and make my way to the front door. When I slip the key into the lock, I notice the impression it has left in my palm, and I hope it remains for just a little bit.

# CHAPTER 4

The massive boxy-headed chocolate Labrador springs from behind the green hopbush and halts a foot to my right. Although I'm not afraid of dogs, my reaction says otherwise as I squeeze what's in my hand, a flimsy plastic cup full of gas station fountain soda. The lid shoots up into the air, and the soda follows like Old Faithful. Stickiness rains down on my hand and arm.

"Ransom, sitzen!" a male voice asserts.

"Why, if it isn't our most favorite visitor," Aunt Paula baby-talks in the massive dog's direction.

The Lab sits, but his tongue is hanging out and over the right side of his bottom teeth, making him look adorable. I've had such an emotional afternoon, and the cuteness is a bit too much to handle. I don't realize it right away, but I'm tearing up.

When I look over at the male standing directly behind the dog, my throat seems to drop into my stomach. The man is dressed in a police uniform, complete with a bulky vest and a K-9 Unit patch on the left and Vernot on the right. And he's insanely good looking, even his ears are handsome. I think for half a second that maybe they're filming some cop drama at Palms Place.

"Sorry about that." The police officer looks down at the dog. "He's selective about listening when he's off the clock. He's trying to decide if he wants to be a good boy or a goodish boy."

That's when I notice the dog is wearing a K-9 tactical vest with the words POLICE across it.

"It's okay. I'm honestly not afraid of him. He just startled me. He's a big Lab." I smile.

"English Lab. Actually, Ransom rarely pokes his nose where it doesn't belong unless Paula is around. Then he turns into a teenager."

"No alligator?" My aunt smiles and glances at me. "Ransom usually carries around his favorite stuffed toy, an alligator."

"It's back in my mom's apartment," the officer says.

"Aaron, I'd like you to meet my niece, Kelly." She turns to me. "Kelly, this is Aaron and the ever-so-handsome Ransom. Marie's son."

I squat down to the dog's level and give him a grin. "English you say?" A British accent I was not aware I had comes out. The dog goes from the perfect sit to some reclined-right-leg-out-relaxed pose. "Nice to meet you, Marie's son. You're furrier than I expected."

"Nice to meet you, Kelly." Aaron chuckles.

I stand. "Nice to meet you, Aaron—" I glance again at his vest "—Vernot. So you speak to your English dog in . . ."

"German. He has a thing for bratwurst." Aaron slides his thumb under the vest, below the radio intercom.

"You know I'm against this." Herbert leans over the balcony. "And look. Now we'll get ants." He speed marches down the steps and points at my drink that's still dripping down my arm.

"It was an accident," I stutter.

"And this dog, he should be a on diet, he's fat." Herbert crosses his arms at his chest.

"He's an English Lab," Aaron and I say in unison even though I'm not sure I understand the difference, other than the dog is rather stocky.

"I don't know what that means," Herbert says.

"It means he's not fat, he's built differently than a regular Lab." Aaron looks down at Ransom who seems to be smiling. "Thicker neck and tail, fuller chest, shorter body and legs, wider head. And they're much calmer than their American counterparts."

Herbert's eyes narrow as he appears to take in the information. "Sorry I called him . . . husky."

"Herbert, we'll clean it up, no worries." Aunt Paula locates a short garden hose by the complex's main entrance and turns it on. "Water will be scalding. Let's give it a second." She waters the two plants nearest her and then tests the water on her finger as Herbert sulks back to his apartment.

I hold my arm out and allow the overly warm water to rinse off the sticky liquid.

"Sorry again about your drink. It was nice to meet you." Aaron looks at Ransom. "*Kommen.*" Aaron and the dog turn in one swift, synced movement. The dog waddles like he's proud to shake his tail fur.

I give a half-hearted wave, as the heat is making me lightheaded.

"You don't look so hot." Aunt Paula takes my left hand.

"Incorrect; I look *very hot.*" I blink the sweat forming around my eyes.

I shuffle behind her as we make our way up the stairs. As we head inside Aunt Paula's apartment, I rejoice as the cool air hits my body. I toss the cup in the trash and give my hands and arms a quick wash with soap in the kitchen sink. Then, like I'm a kid, I sprawl out on the carpet under the ceiling fan as it pushes the cold air around the room.

"I need to shower." Aunt Paula stands over me, her gray hair *whooshes* forward, covering her ears. "Shoot, I forgot. If you have a hankering for ice cream tonight, we're out."

"I can run to the store." I ease up onto my elbows. "I'm leaving tomorrow around lunchtime, so if you have a grocery list, I can knock it out for you." I flash back to the memories of our trips to the grocery store, her buying me bubble gum and *BOP* magazines.

Aunt Paula sticks her hand to her hip. "I can't believe you have to leave already. Seems like you just got here."

"It does." It was already Saturday afternoon. "I'm sorry I can't stay longer. But I promise I'll be here for the holidays."

She half smiles. "Sure, that would be nice."

As I stand, she heads down the hall and peeks her head back out around the wall. "The list is on the refrigerator, and the insulated bag is hanging in the pantry."

"Is there a specific store you want me to go to?" I move into the kitchen, grab the list under the magnet, and locate the insulated bag. Without it, half the ice cream would melt walking from the store to the car.

"Fry's is fine," Aunt Paula calls from the bathroom.

I remove my phone from my back pocket and check the temperature—112. I'll be lucky if I don't melt walking to my car. After grabbing a water bottle, I head out, locking the door behind me. When I reach the bottom of the exterior stairs, I spot a familiar resident in the courtyard but don't recall her name. She's wearing a floral skirt, white blouse, and wedge sandals, and she's carrying a Boston terrier.

"Good afternoon!" she calls out when she spots me.

"You have a dog? You better not let Herbert see it," I mention.

"Rosa, number two." She halts and the dog is panting harshly.

"Is he okay?" I reach out to touch his head.

"Now he is. Or she." Rosa lifts the dog. "She. She is okay now." Rosa looks over her shoulder toward Herbert's apartment. "I stole her."

"What?" My head snaps forward. Her ability to casually admit she stole an animal is unexpected.

"When you leave a dog in a car. In the summer, Rosa, will break into your car. And take it. After the police came out, I'm very convincing to the horrible owner, and she gives up the dog."

My mouth falls open, and I must look like the mask from *Scream*. "Oh, how'd you do that?"

"Police fine her, and she is wailing, making a very big scene. After police leave, I tell her she can make it right in God's eyes by giving me the dog."

"Rosa!" I give the Boston terrier a long pet from his neck to his tail. "She's a cutie."

"I lied, just to get the dog away, because the law should be more than money or short stay in the lockup. I can't keep her. Palms Place has a no pet rule." Rosa sighs. "Ah, but you can." She hoists the dog toward me. "You need a dog."

I shake my head. "My life is a little complicated right now. Plus, I have one back home."

She squints and nods her head, pulling the dog back to her chest. "Shucks. I must get her some more water and cool her." She heads towards her front door and gives a wave.

I glance to see if Herbert is looking out his window, and though I'm happy Rosa saved the dog, I worry Herbert will blow a gasket if he spots the Boston terrier.

As I walk to my Nissan Rogue, I can't help but feel like the rubber is melting on the bottom of my flip-flops. Once I start the engine, I place my hands on the steering wheel and squeal. I check my palms, making sure there are no burn marks. Tomorrow can't come quick enough. I've spent more than *enough* time in the valley this summer.

Somehow, my grocery shopping turned into a shopping spree. And I refuse to make a second trip back to the car, so it takes a few tries to balance the bags and heave them up the flight of stairs to Aunt Paula's apartment. I unlock the door, and as I kick it open, the bags slip from my grasp, crashing onto the carpet in the living room. Red lines cross my palms from the impressions of the handles.

"Aunt Paula?" I expect her to be out of the shower by now, but I still hear the water running. "Sorry I took so long. The woman in front of me was writing . . . *a check*."

I collect the bags and drag them into the kitchen, leaving them on the floor by the peninsula. "Aunt Paula?"

"Kelly!"

I go toward the hall. The bathroom door is closed, and panic bubbles up in my chest as I knock. "Aunt Paula?"

"Kelly."

I grip the doorknob. "Can I come in?"

Silence. "Yes."

I ease it open and steam filters out.

"I fell." Aunt Paula is lying in the tub with the flamingo shower curtain covering the top of her as the water shoots from the showerhead. "Dare I say it? I can't get up." She sobs. "I'm *that* commercial."

I gasp at the sight and reach into the shower, turning off the water. "Aunt Paula, oh my gosh, are you alright? Do you want me to call 911?"

"I don't know. I think I broke my ankle."

I glance down and notice her left foot appears swollen and discolored, but thankfully, no bones are protruding out of her skin. "Hopefully it's just a sprain and or a mild fracture. I don't think it's broken. You'd be screaming, and I would've passed out from seeing it." I remove my cell phone from my pocket. "Let me call the paramedics."

Tears roll down her cheeks. "Kelly." Aunt Paula glances at herself and the shower curtain. "They can't see me naked."

"I'll figure out something." I glance at the plush peach-colored towel on the rack, knowing that won't be enough.

"Oh, no." She brings her hand to her face. "How are they going to get me out of here? Everyone will see me. Every single resident will see me . . . like this."

"I'm sorry. We'll try to figure something out." But we knew that was a lie. There was no way to shield this accident from the nosy Palms Place residents.

# CHAPTER 5

"Absolutely not," Aunt Paula says from the emergency room bed at Banner Del E. Webb. "No, I won't let you."

"You don't have to *let me*. It's my choice." I take her hand in mine as I sit on the edge of the bed.

There is continuous beeping out in the hall, beyond the room's door, which makes for a very unsettling atmosphere. Then there's a louder beep coming from somewhere down the hall. "Code pink to pediatrics. Code pink to pediatrics."

We glance at each other, unsure of what code pink means, but it doesn't sound good. I'm grateful I can be here for my aunt but also wish I knew some of the staff. In Flag, I'm well connected with the social workers in hospitals and rehab centers, making it easier to get anything I need handled. Everyone at Del Webb is a stranger to us both.

I check the analog clock on the wall. It's six in the evening, and my aunt has yet to see a doctor. Thankfully, we were put into a room as soon as we arrived. The nurse came in and took the basics, followed by two ladies who did an X-ray without her having to leave the room or her bed. Right after that, they wheeled her in to get a CT scan of the ankle joint, but we're still waiting for the results. I had to admit that everything was running mor e efficiently than I expected. Aunt Paula's eyes are heavy, probably from the pain medication. Thankfully, they had her medical history from the other Banner she went to back when she was attacked with a knife. So, they gave her oxycodone since she's allergic to morphine. I shiver. The hospital must have their air conditioning set in the high sixties.

"Kelly, I said no." Aunt Paula crosses her arms over her chest.

I shift on the bed, moving my knee closer to her hip as the rough bleached sheet twists under me. "It's not up for discussion. I've already called and left a message with my manager."

"Missing work will only make things worse for you. Besides, if your department is short-staffed, who is going to cover for you?"

"We've been short-staffed for the last five years. And I have plenty of vacation time, sick time, and even family leave time I can use."

"You're supposed to use that time to spend with Drew, trying to work through things. Or at the very least, relax."

*Drew.* We'd only texted a handful of times since I left. My thoughts travel into the past, when his face was adorably unshaved and he had messy bed hair. The way he'd lean his shoulder on the doorjamb, sipping his coffee and smiling at me . . . But then it fades, because he hasn't looked at me like that in years.

I blink and scrunch up my nose. "I'm supposed to take care of you."

Aunt Paula uncrosses her arms and lets out a deep, loud sigh. "Fine, then, I guess. Now's a good time to tell me about Drew."

I look around, avoiding eye contact. She's right; I can't escape. She knows I wouldn't leave her alone in the ER.

"There is really nothing to tell. I asked him if he slept with her and he said no, it was only talking."

"And you believe Drew?"

"Yes . . ." I lower my chin and gaze down at my hands. "I'm not sure. I don't know what to believe. Especially because of how I found out."

"How did you find out? You never mentioned it. Did you find it on his phone?"

"Joey."

"Your dog ratted him out? How is that possible?"

"Remember, Joey is *his* dog. *His* best friend. *His* person. Joey tolerates me." I wrap my hand around my fist and squeeze. "We were out walking one evening, and I decided I wanted ice cream from this cute little shop off Aspen Way. Well, Joey suddenly acts like he knows this younger woman who's clearly trying to avoid being seen. But she couldn't escape because there was a bit of a crowd on the sidewalk. And I know how Joey acts when he sees someone he knows. His tail was full speed, turbo wagging. He was lunging on his leash, trying to get to her. When we got close enough, I noticed the way she glanced at Drew and how his eyes were all jetting around with avoidance. Something just felt . . . off.

"She bent down to give Joey a pet, still acting like it was the first time she met the dog. And they seemed as though they didn't know who should say something first. So, I finally caved and asked if they knew each other. After a long silence, Drew mentioned they knew each other from Gamblers Anonymous. Yet, Joey has never gone with him to a meeting. He's not a service dog. Drew then said it was at a barbecue afterwards, when he brought Joey. But he stumbled over his words like two left feet. And then he admitted they'd been hanging out as friends. Friends don't act like that around each other, nor do they hide each other from their spouses."

Aunt Paula goes white, and her mouth falls ajar. "Oh, Kelly." She shakes her head. "And all this time, you thought he was going to group to overcome his addiction."

"I should have sent him to Liars Anonymous." I wipe a tear that threatens to fall.

"What a shame," a voice comes from the door. "My goodness, what is this world coming to? If it were my son"—the nurse comes further into the room, her black Crocs squeaking louder on the floor with each step closer to the bed—"I would've slapped him right upside the head." She pushes the button on the wall. "What do you need, sugar?"

"Oh, we're okay . . ." Aunt Paula peeks at the nurse's ID tag. "Bonnie."

"Well, you hit the call light on the remote." Bonnie points at the bed.

I stand as my aunt shifts her bottom, and the nurse pulls a cord attached to a smorgasbord of buttons, including the ability to control the TV.

"Pain medication is working. You didn't even know you were sitting on it." Bonnie laughs. "I'd say that dog did you a favor."

I give a half-hearted smile. "Yep, dogs are as honest as five-year-olds."

"Like I always say, you can trust a dog more than you can trust a person." The nurse clips the remote device around the bedrail. "Alight, sugar, hopefully the doc will be with you soon so you can get discharged."

The light above the door across the way flashes, and the nurse notices it. "Just remember, no one is perfect." Bonnie hurries out of the room.

"She has a point." Aunt Paula adjusts her hands and weaves her fingers together on her lap.

"I'm not perfect, nor is he, but there's a line you shouldn't cross."

"How are you doing at the house?"

"I'm in the main bedroom, and he's in the guestroom. Neither of us can afford to move out."

It's when I pause that I notice Aunt Paula has tears in her eyes. "Do you still love him?"

"Yes, I do." I take her hand. "Aunt Paula, are you okay?"

She wipes a tear before it rolls further down her cheek. "That's good. Some people deserve to be forgiven."

I tilt my head. These words feel like more than just words, like emotions, experiences. "Did Steve cheat on you? No"—I pinch my eyes closed—"no, not Andrew."

"No." She shakes her head. "I . . . I was unfaithful when I was married to Andrew."

It's a good thing I'm already in the emergency room, because my heart just dropped on the floor. My perfect aunt, who reminds me of June Cleaver, just said she cheated on the love of her life. I'm hot, sweat forms, and nausea rises in the back of my throat. The room starts to look fuzzy, as I can hear my heartbeat thumping in my ears. Then, everything goes dark.

When I come to, I see Nurse Bonnie leaning over me. "You're okay, sugar. Take it easy."

I try to sit up and realize I'm already at an incline, I'm on a bed. When I glance around and notice I'm in my own room, alone, I touch my neck, feeling a foam collar around it.

"Oh gosh, what happened?"

"I guess you wanted your own bed." Bonnie adjusts the pulsometer on my pointer finger.

I grab at my neck again. "What's this for?"

"The foam collar is only a precaution. You can take it off in twenty-four hours."

"I'm fine." I wave off the nurse.

"You will be." Bonnie snaps up the left bedrail. "Rest up."

"But my aunt. I need to be with her."

Bonnie stops at the door frame and looks at her watch. "Okay, sugar, but take my hand." She lowers the bedrail, unhooks me from the devices—including the blood pressure monitor—and walks with me next door to my aunt's room.

"That was scary, Kelly. Don't ever do that again." Aunt Paula wags her finger at me.

I try to wave the nurse and my aunt off. "I'm fine. This is about her." I point at my aunt. "She's the one in pain. She's the one that's hurt."

Bonnie chuckles. "If the good Lord hadn't made my feet so fast, your head would've hit the ground."

"She caught you before you hit the floor, but your neck took a little whiplash when you careened into her bosom," Aunt Paula mentions.

"Yeah, God went a little overboard on my upper voluptuousness, and unfortunately, it caused a bit of ricochet for your head." Bonnie grins.

I cover my mouth, thinking about how that must have looked. Aunt Paula and Bonnie share a laugh as Bonnie makes me sit down in the chair next to my aunt's bed.

"I'll let you two have some privacy now. Drink your juice." Bonnie points at the little jug of apple juice on the bedside tray and hurries out of the room, taking the squeakiness of her Crocs with her.

"Sorry I made you pass out." Aunt Paula presses her lips together.

"It's my fault. I'm starving, probably low blood sugar." I open the container and take a long sip. The coolness travels down my throat.

"Let's change the subject. I want to go home and don't want another reason to stay here. So, what do you think your boss is going to say about you staying in Sun City?"

"I have no clue. My coworkers won't be happy. I had a full week of meetings scheduled, so they'll have to reschedule them or try to find coverage."

"Alrighty, I'm Dr. Anderson." An insanely tall version of Danny DeVito, as though he'd been stretched out like Silly Putty, steps into the room with a tablet in his hand. His balding head has a crescent moon patch of dark brown hair at his ears. He adjusts his glasses, but somehow, they remain crooked on his nose. Dr. Anderson doesn't shake our hands. "Your CT scan and X-rays show acute mildly comminuted non-displaced oblique fracture of the metaphysis and proximal diaphysis of the fibula and multiple small non-displaced fractures of the ankle and foot."

We blink at Mr. DeVito, aka Dr. Anderson, as he glances up from his tablet.

"Can you repeat that in layman's terms?" Aunt Paula asks.

"You have a non-displaced chip fracture." He swipes on the tablet with his middle finger.

"Non-displaced is good, Aunt Paula," I say. "It means your bones are not out of place."

"Right, it also means no surgery. But you'll need to follow up with the outpatient ortho as soon as possible. Until then, it's non-weight-bearing. We'll get you set up in a walking boot, although, for the time being, you can't walk on it." He swipes on the tablet again. "And your ortho doc will get you set up with the process, PT, etcetera. You have care at home, correct?"

"Correct. I'll be just fine at home."

Dr. Anderson side-eyes me with his disapproval.

"I'll be managing her care, so it's still a safe discharge," I inform the doctor.

"Alrighty then. You gals have a nice rest of your day." He turns smoothly as his long white coat blows like a cape behind him, and heads back into the hall.

Aunt Paula looks down at her foot and sighs. "Honestly, Kel, I can't ask you to stay, and I don't expect you to, either. I *can* manage on my own."

"I don't want to hear it. If my job is to make sure others get the care they need, then I most certainly need to make sure my family does, too. You're all I have."

"You have Drew."

"Do I?" I take her hand again in mine and run my thumb over her soft-but-paper-thin skin. "Right now, all that matters is *you*."

Tears form on the rims of Aunt Paula's eyes. "I appreciate you. Thank you."

She's a private person who doesn't like to ask for help. And who knows how long she would have remained in that tub, refusing to call out for help from a neighbor. However, I selfishly hope that by taking time off, it'll upset my manager enough that they'll fire me. Although it would be catastrophic, I could finally set myself free of a job I no longer love and that I'm too afraid to leave. I loved it when I started, before management twisted and pulled us to do more without the needed resources. I've been burned-out for several years. And there is no way I can bring myself to leave the position for something else. I'm too scared. I hate change, and there are too many unknowns with a new job. The grass isn't always greener on the other side.

"Kelly?"

I snap out of my thoughts and blink. "Sorry, I was just thinking." The sounds of the busy hospital rush back to my ears, and the random beeps outside the room return. "What do you do if you enjoy the main aspect of your job but not the changes that have turned it into the opposite of what it once was? Nothing is perfect, but it should be better than it is."

Aunt Paula attempts to shift in the bed but doesn't get very far. "Listen, Kel, I understand your frustration. Yet, in life, there will always be things you can't change. You need to think about if you can or should continue to allow it to eat away at you, or if you can accept it and move past it. If your mom were here, she'd never want you to live with this cloud over your head. Be it in your marriage or your career. She would support any decision you made that was best for you." Aunt Paula scratches her half-washed hair. "All she ever wanted was for you to be happy. From the moment she found out she was pregnant with you, all she talked about was raising you to believe in yourself and live a happy life."

I bite the inside of my cheek as my bottom lip quivers.

"You know, I've always believed there is a reason for everything in life. Although I would've preferred to not have fallen in the shower, there was a reason I did. I know it in my heart, I can feel it."

"What you feel is the fracture." I squeeze her hand. "You didn't need to injure yourself."

"I think I did. I've asked you to come and see me many times. But a person can only nag so much."

"I'm good with excuses."

"Sometimes our weaknesses are really our strengths, and strengths are really weaknesses. Just because we're alive doesn't mean we are actually living."

# Chapter 6

"Why does this place not have an elevator?" I come around the front of the Nissan. "I don't have any idea how I'm going to get her up those stairs."

"What happened to your neck, Ms. Kelly?" Herbert meets me at the passenger door.

"She hit a bosom." Aunt Paula laughs.

"On purpose?" Herbert adjusts his worn vet's hat.

"No, Herbert," I whine. "Not on purpose."

"Why didn't you get medical transportation to bring you home?" Herbert's wearing a faded blue T-shirt with VETERAN written in red, white, and dark blue across it.

"Her insurance didn't cover it." I ponder the situation by crossing my arms, because usually that helps.

"I'm already in debt from the ambulance ride and the ER visit deductible. Insurance only covers so much," Aunt Paula adds.

"Ah, yes, those deductibles have a habit of biting you in the rump." Herbert scratches the back of his neck. "Maybe we can hook up some sort of pulley system?"

I stopped at Goodwill on the way home in search of crutches, because the cost of getting them from the hospital was insane, even with insurance. I was lucky to find a decent pair, but there's no way Aunt Paula can maneuver them on steps.

"We need someone to carry you up the stairs." I glance at Palms Place through the open gate.

"We're just glad you're okay, Ms. Paula. You gave us all a scare when the ambulance pulled in." Herbert sighs as though he was traumatized.

"What happened, Kelly?" Rosa appears behind Herbert, along with what remains of a cigarette between her pointer and middle finger.

"She hit bosoms," Herbert says, and Rosa nods her head like this is a familiar outcome.

"Stop crowding around. I have Kelly to help me." Aunt Paula tries to rotate her bottom on the passenger seat.

"But she leaves, right?" Rosa's accent causes it to sound like an accusation rather than a question.

"I'm staying." I try to wrangle Aunt Paula's feet onto the pavement below. She has a walking boot on her left foot, and she isn't supposed to put any weight on it. I remove the crutches from the back seat, but still need to get them under her arms.

I huff and assess the situation, then mimic putting the crutches under her armpits, attempting to figure it out. I try to angle out and up, then shake the crutches in frustration. I glance at Herbert and Rosa. They aren't old, but they're not young either. The last thing I need is a second trip to Del Webb on my to-do-list.

"Rosa, can you hold these please?" I hand her the crutches before she can respond.

"Aunt Paula, I'm going to bear hug you to stand, and then we can get the crutches in place." I move directly in front of her and bend forward, my bottom smacking into the passenger door.

"I feel ridiculous," Aunt Paula says into my shoulder as I count.

"One, well don't, two, three." I hoist her up and forward, so her head clears the frame of the door. Rosa, in her wedged heels, claps on the concrete as she steps forward and shoves the crutches at us.

Once Aunt Paula is balanced with a crutch under each arm, I grab our purses and lock my car. Then I follow beside her as I've seen so many caregivers do. We move closer to the pool in the middle of Palms Place's courtyard, and residents open their front doors. It feels like an attack, an overwhelming chaos of voices and feet. And it reminds me of the time I ran out of a meeting at a mental health center to protect myself from a client chasing me through the halls. The residents approach in a blur of faces and chattering. I release a breath to try and slow my heart rate down.

"I'm fine. Don't treat me as though I'm dying." Aunt Paula raises her voice over the commotion.

"I've got a casserole in my refrigerator for you," a resident says.

"Let me know if you need anything," another says. "Kelly, what happened to your neck?"

"Calcium cannon accident," Herbert announces.

My aunt and I reach the bottom of the exterior stairs that'll take us to the second level, and we look at each other as though unsure about the stairs and Herbert's word choice.

Herbert approaches on my right. "See, I told you. You need a pulley system." He leans back, his hands on his hips, and gazes up the stairs like it's the Empire State Building.

"What about Aaron?" Rosa raises her right eyebrow, along with her cigarette.

"What about me?" a male voice comes over the crowd.

I attempt to turn my head to the left, but don't get very far with the collar. So, I turn my entire body, and see the police officer, without Ransom, holding a garbage bag, exiting his mom's apartment.

"Mr. Aaron, do you have any devices in your cruiser that we can use to get Ms. Paula up to her apartment?" Herbert asks over the top of our heads.

"I'm not a construction worker," Aaron responds in a sharp, authoritative tone.

"Do you have *any* ideas about how we can get her up the stairs?" I assume he has at least a little rescue experience.

"What happened to your neck?" Aaron points at me.

"Bosom accident," Rosa says.

Aaron shrugs, apparently satisfied with no need for more information, and moves toward the exit of Palms Place. "The stairs are too narrow for a person on both sides of her."

I wonder if he's thinking the same as I am. Narrow stairs or not, Aaron and I are the least likely to break a hip trying to get her up them. Stairs are dangerous even with young hips.

I stand there, and when Aaron returns, I leave my aunt's side and approach him. "There's no way you can help us?"

He looks over my shoulder at the stairs but says nothing.

"We're the youngest ones here. I might not be the strongest, but we're about the same height."

Aaron raises his eyebrow at me.

"It's not an insult, it's a fact. If you were taller, or if I was shorter, she'd lean like a one-legged stool."

He glances at my aunt and then up the stairs again. "It's fine. I can manage on my own."

"What? Look, it's been a long day. And I don't think the attitude is necessary." I hurry after Grumpy Cop.

"No need." He stands in front of Aunt Paula. "Ready for a bumpy ride?"

My aunt's face contorts with confusion.

"Alright." He claps his hands once and bends down. "Hold on."

The crutches fly outward, and my aunt lets out a squeal as Aaron flings her over his shoulder in a fireman's carry.

My arms reach forward and catch one crutch, but the other bounces off the concrete below. Scooping it up, I follow them up the stairs. My aunt's hair springs with each step Aaron takes. Once at the top of the landing, he lowers her, holding her at the elbows until I get the crutches under her.

By the time we secure the crutches in place, he's at the bottom of the stairs.

"Aaron," I call down. "Thank you."

The rest of the Palms Place residents are staring, mouths slightly ajar. Aaron waves a hand in the air and mumbles something. I wonder if he's always this grumpy, or maybe he just had a bad day. Then I recall times when I despised social interaction after dealing with the public all day.

"That was a rush." Aunt Paula shakes her head, and her hair falls back into place. "The perks of being injured, handsome men carrying me." She elbows me.

"I think the pain medication is talking. Come on, let's get inside. I'm dehydrated just being out here." I jam my key into the apartment door. "How hot is it today?"

"I think it's only 109." She says it as though 109 is 76 degrees.

Shutting the door behind us, Aunt Paula wobbles as she nears the recliner. I drop our purses at my feet and run to her, catching her by the arm.

"I'm fine, Kel." Her hand reaches for her recliner and the crutch under her right arm drops to the carpet.

I try to nod my head, but the foam collar prevents it. "Sure, sure." I help her turn around and lower into the chair. "I'll get you a nice glass of ice water."

"Can you put the ice in a strawberry daiquiri?"

"You're on pain medication," I call out from the kitchen. "That'll have to wait."

"Well, how are we supposed to have a party?"

"Party?"

"If you're bent on staying, although I can manage just fine, then shouldn't we have a party? I mean, won't this be your first vacation in . . . years?"

"I went on vacation last Christmas." I enter the living room and hand her a glass of ice water and take a big gulp from my own glass.

"You spent one night at the Grand Canyon."

"It's not my fault. We could only afford one night." I ease into the couch and close my eyes. I pull up the memory of the historic hotel with the view overlooking the canyon. Not that Drew and I took in much of the view. I had a work call that he asked me not to take, but he did. So later we fought and then spent the night on the edge of the bed like two four-year-olds perfecting the silent treatment.

"Why didn't you just ask me?" Aunt Paula lowers the glass onto the side table.

"Ask you for what?" I allow the ice cube to rest on my upper lip, holding the glass to it.

"I might be on a fixed income, but I can still help you enjoy life."

My cheeks flush because I'm forty-two and should be in a better spot financially, and I find it embarrassing. "No, Aunt Paula. I'm fine."

"Kel, are you sure you can stay?" Her eyes flicker with sleepiness.

I sit silently and turn to the dark TV screen. I can't form the words I want to say. They're jumbled and piled up in the corner of my mind. All I can think about is how I'm failing at everything in life. And also, I'm trying to understand how my lovely aunt could have cheated on my sweet uncle.

"Kelly?"

The living room has grown dark and the only light coming in is through the open blinds near the kitchen table. "Of course, stop asking me. I can stay, no worries. Can we please forget about the world for a bit? I've had my fill."

"Okay."

"Thank you." But I can't shut off my mind. I want answers about why she cheated. I also want answers about why Drew cheated. Maybe understanding why my aunt did it will help me forgive Drew.

"How about we have supper?" Aunt Paula's voice breaks through my thoughts like a plane emerging from the clouds.

"Oh, gosh, yes, it's late. Let's see what I can make."

"No need. Remember, Vivian said she had a casserole?"

There's a knock at the door, and we look at each other. I take a few steps and open it. Immediately, I want to close it as the late evening heat engulfs me. Instead, I smile half-heartedly.

"*Bonjour*, I hope you're hungry!" Vivian wiggles the glass dish in front of my face. "*No, no*, don't just stand there with the door open. You're going to let all the heat in."

I stumble out of the way, resting my hand on my foam collar as Vivian dashes inside and I slam the door shut.

"Paula, how do you feel?" Vivian moves about the apartment as though it's hers. Then I realize every apartment at Palms Place has the same layout.

"I'll be fine. Thank you dearly for bringing food over. Kelly and I are not up for cooking tonight."

"*Oui*, especially in this heat. Anything to keep the oven off." Vivian sets the dish on the peninsula. "This is the most delectable cold casserole ever!"

"Please tell me it's your delicious dill tuna noodle casserole?" Aunt Paula sits forward in her recliner.

My mouth waters at the name.

"*Oui*, the one and only." Vivian heads back towards the door. "*Au revoir.*"

"You're not going to stay?" I eye my aunt to make sure she even wants company.

"Heavens no." Vivian flickers her wrist. "I'm going to sit in the pool. If I don't get at least ten minutes in the water this time of year, I dry up like an apricot. Wrinklier than God and time has already made me." Vivian reaches for the doorknob. "If you ladies need anything, just let me know."

She swings the door open, and Herbert nearly falls into Vivian. They appear to dance the tango and before I realize what's happening, Vivian is gone, and Hebert is standing in the living room with the door closed behind him.

"Golly, it's another scorcher out there, right, ladies?" Herbert's posture is so straight I worry he's secretly a robot.

"What can we do for you, Herbert?" Aunt Paula leans forward in her recliner.

"I wanted to make sure you knew that I'm here to do anything that needs doing. Outside of that muscular-young-man stunt from Mr. Aaron earlier, I don't suspect Ms. Maria's kid will be of much help. He's too busy handling that chocolate beast."

"Now, Herbert, be nice." Aunt Paula folds her arms over her lap and interlaces her fingers. "Service animals are allowed, and Ransom is the sweetest dog on the planet. We get a cop and K-9 protection. Besides, Aaron will only be here for a short time."

"A month is far from a short time. I sincerely hope you're not taking sides, Ms. Paula. Fur is fur, service or not." Herbert's chin draws up toward the ceiling fan. "Now, I want to reiterate my willingness to assist you."

"Why don't you join us for some of Vivian's casserole?" My Aunt gestures at the counter where the foil-covered glass dish sits.

"Thank you, kindly, but I won't intrude on your time together, let alone your need for rest. I shall be on my way. Just know I'm only a shout away." He turns toward the door. "Or I suspect, a knock away."

Before I can finish blinking, Aunt Paula's neighbor is out the front door. The blast of heat smacks my side, and my eyes widen. "I don't know how you do it." I glance up at the ceiling fan and say a grateful prayer.

"Well, we don't go on and on about it," Aunt Paula says. "I'm starving."

I cringe and move to the kitchen, removing the foil. The aroma of dill and tuna and whatever else is in this dish causes my mouth to water. I'm so happy I don't have to cook or plan a meal. Thinking of something to make night after night is always such a challenge for me. There were only so many ways to dress up chicken or turkey. And while Drew offered to cook, canned soup or hot dogs never grew on me.

I take our plates into the living room and hand her the plate with a fork shoved into the casserole.

"Can I get you something else to drink? Tea?"

"My daiquiri?"

"Nice try. We'll have plenty of time for that once you're off your pain medications."

"You'll be staying that long?"

"I'm not sure. I'll have a better idea after speaking with my boss." With my plate, I lower onto the couch, folding my legs under my bottom.

"What shall we watch? Maybe something down memory lane?"

"Sounds great."

She points the remote at the TV, and it comes to life. She flips through some channels before *Three's Company* appears on the screen. "Remember how much you loved this show?"

I hold my fork in front of my mouth, which is full of casserole. "Yes." I think of how often Drew and I watched reruns of it late at night, and it makes it hard to swallow as the emotions surface.

"Who would've thought me fracturing my ankle would mean I get to spend extra time with my favorite niece?"

"I'm your only niece." I awkwardly glance at her, pivoting my entire upper body, and see a sneaky smile form on her face. But my smile quickly fades because I know this *wouldn't* have happened if she hadn't hurt herself. And it reminds me I have some changes to make once I figure out how.

# CHAPTER 7

I'm leaning on the railing of the terrace overlooking the courtyard when I end the call with my manager back in Flag. The sun is already peeking over the '70s-style single-story homes of Sun City, and my sunglasses do little to lessen the glare off the metal air-conditioning units mounted on the nearby house roofs. I run my hand along the back of my neck. It's a little sore, which the doctor said would be normal, but at least I don't have to wear that foam collar anymore. Who would have thought someone else's chest would be so dangerous?

The pool's water is as still as the surface of a forgotten lake. Locusts are buzzing in the trees, and it's numbing to my ears. The view of the mountains in every direction is a beautiful distraction for a few seconds. The desert has so much to offer, if you take the time to see it.

"Good morning, Ms. Kelly," a familiar male voice says upon a front door easing open to my right.

I clutch my cell phone, stand upright, and turn to see Herbert. He's holding a black coffee mug with *Marine Corps* etched on it in white. Steam rises from the pure black liquid. "What a splendid morning. Did you hear the high is only going to be 107 today?"

"Sounds better than 113." My shirt is already sticking to my back from the sweat. "How can you drink hot coffee?" I point to his cup.

Herbert glances down at the mug and back up at me with a grin. "Have you tasted cold coffee, even with cream and sugar? I would rather lick a metal pole. Simple bold black coffee, nothing to mask the flavor of a quality bean."

"I see." I make my way to my aunt's front door and reach for the knob. "Have a good day."

"You know, Ms. Kelly, I think it's a good thing you're sticking around for Ms. Paula. But it's unnecessary. We can all pitch in."

"I'm sure she appreciates the thought; I know I do. She's lucky to have all of you."

"I just want to make sure that because of your extended stay, the rules will continue to be followed. We know Mr. Aaron won't be enforcing them."

"Enforce?" My hand grips the doorknob.

"Yes, the rules for Palms Place. Curfews on noise, no strange people overnight, no loitering."

I chuckle. "I'm none of those things, Herbert. And as for Aaron and his K-9, I'm sure he puts in long, exhausting hours. Maybe cut him a little slack?"

"We don't want it to get all willy-nilly around here. That's how things go from good to bad. People doing whatever they please." He raises his mug to his mouth and takes a long slurp.

"I'll do my best not to cause a ruckus. Have a nice day, Herbert." I open the door and close it with my fist in a tight ball.

I wasn't here to make friends, but I wasn't here to make enemies, either. And I was far from being willy-nilly.

"Is everything alright?" Aunt Paula asks from her recliner.

"I'm sorry. Did I wake you?" I glance at the time on my cell phone.

"No, not at all. I'm usually up much earlier than this, getting in my walk before the sun comes up."

Aunt Paula spent the night in her recliner. She couldn't get comfortable in her bed with her foot raised, so after ten minutes of us getting frustrated trying to get her set, she ended up back in the living room.

"I take it all is well with your supervisor?" she asks suspiciously.

"Yes, and she wanted me to thank you for your accident."

Aunt Paula moves forward in her chair, and I rush to her, hoisting her under the arm to stand. I reach for the crutches leaning against the wall while still holding onto her arm. "And why is that?"

"Turns out the offices in Maricopa County have an insane turnover rate, even higher than in Coconino County. Plus, they're short-staffed too."

"I'm confused. How will that work?" She rests her upper body on the crutches and moves toward the bathroom.

"Since we're doing fieldwork, we're not tethered to a certain office. Job duties are the same across the state. The only difference is the population we serve and the different levels of available services. In Flag, some workers speak Navajo, and down here, they have Spanish-speaking workers. Being bilingual is not a requirement, but it helps." I follow behind her as she keeps trying to wave me off.

"And what does that mean for you?" She reaches the bathroom door.

"I'm taking a caseload of clients in Sun City and the surrounding cities. I'll be out for meetings, but I can be back throughout the day to make sure you have everything you need."

"That sounds like a lot more work than you need to deal with." She hands me the crutches as she grabs the counter, preventing me from coming all the way into the bathroom to help her.

"It's the same job I normally do. I just don't know the area well or any staff at the facilities. She's allowing me to take today to set up for the week ahead. Schedule meetings and adjust my calendar." Aunt Paula closes the door. "I'm here to help if you need anything," I call through the door.

"Trust me, I'm aware. I'm fine."

"Maybe you want to take a shower?" I rest my forehead on the door.

"Perhaps, later."

There is no ceiling fan to push the cooler air around in the hall, so it's warmer than the rest of the apartment. I need to put on a calm face because I don't want Aunt Paula to realize I'm sort of freaking out about doing my job here. Sure, it's the same, but it's also not. It's out of my comfort zone. And I hate that. I avoid it at all costs. It's why I go to the same grocery store every week. It's why I refuse to go to a different Costco when I'm near one after work because every store's layout is different, and I frankly don't have time for that nightmare. I don't want to search all over because someone put the noodles on a different aisle.

"Maybe you should've told your boss you were under the weather and taken sick time," Aunt Paula says through the door.

"I have a lot of hours to use, but anything over two days and I need a doctor's note."

The bathroom door pops open. "Well, Kel, this is a retirement community. Consider us the Amazon of doctor's notes." Her eyes widen, and with arched brows, a scandalous look passes across her face.

"I've never lied for work!" I exclaim at the inference that she thought I'd be okay with it.

"Never?" She takes the crutches from me and hobbles to the kitchen.

"Never." I scurry after her. "Where are you going?"

"Never ever?" She pauses at the refrigerator.

"Okay, I took a stack of sticky notes and the super nice gel pens." I stand in front of her, blocking her from squeezing between me and the refrigerator.

"I knew it. You have *office supply thief* written all over you." Aunt Paula eyes me and heaves a sigh as I gasp. "Now move, please. I'm starving."

A knock at the front door causes us to both turn our heads.

"Go sit down. I'll fix your breakfast." I point at the kitchen table and hurry to the door.

I open it without looking through the peephole. "Herbert?"

"Apologies for the interruption, Ms. Kelly, but were you aware that Ms. Rosa has a dog?"

I peek around him as though they're nearby. "No, I'm not aware of an animal."

Aunt Paula clears her throat, and I kick my leg back as though to tell her to hush.

"I wanted to bring it up with Ms. Maria's son, but he's not answering the door. I believe he's on the wrong side of the rules, anyway, with his police dog."

"And you came here because?" I lean on the door.

"You're the youngest person at Palms Place. The one with the most spring in your step. You have authority and youth in your veins." Herbert shoved his hands in his front jean pockets.

"I appreciate the compliment, I think." My eyes narrow, questioning if he meant it as such. "However, I'm only here to care for my aunt and work."

"You're working?" Carol, from the other side of the terrace, calls out.

"How did she hear that?" I whisper.

"She has those top-of-the-line hearing aids. She can hear me playing the *trombone* in my bathroom, if you catch my drift." Herbert steps aside.

"Herbert!" Aunt Paula groans over my shoulder.

Carol has a bag of trash in her hand, as she gracefully makes her way over.

"What is it you do again?" Carol asks, dressed in khaki pants and a pale-blue blouse.

"I'm a social worker, in the medical field."

"Medical, great." Carol pulls aside the corner of her blouse. "Can you look at this rash I have?"

"Carol, I'm not a doctor or a nurse. I can't diagnose anything." I don't look away; I've learned a trick or two over the years. People love to have answers to what ails them, and I don't have the stomach or knowledge for it. But if people catch you seeming to be unsympathetic, it opens a can of worms. So, I focus on something else nearby when I'm supposed to look and try to blur everything else out.

"But you've seen rashes and such before. What do you think?" Carol points at her stomach.

Carol is correct, I can usually determine if someone has C. diff or if a UTI is causing dementia-like behaviors, but I dare not mention it aloud. I've professionally gained knowledge, but not a degree, and I could lose my job by giving out advice. Reviewing medical records and learning very intimate health information about people's lives has taught me where our basic problems lie. If you want to see your community unfiltered, become a social worker. Regardless of being rich, poor, or middle class, they all face the same angels and demons when it comes to their bodies.

"Kelly? Does it look bad?" Carol asks again.

I can't help but peek this time, because she's not leaving without some sort of answer. "Have you switched detergents or soaps? Even something you've used a thousand times over?"

"I don't think so."

"Have you checked the ingredients in a while? Sometimes companies will change them without the consumer being alerted. Also, you can develop an allergy to something that you were once okay with. If you have an old bottle of anything, double-check it with the new one, and if you have the time, see if anyone is talking about it online. The internet is notorious for calling out changes. Just a month ago, I started having a food allergy to a granola bar I'd been eating for several years. Turns out they swapped coconut oil for soybean oil."

"Thank you. I knew you'd have a solution. I tried to show it to Aaron, him being a cop, I'm sure he sees rashes, but he told me to go to urgent care if I was worried." Carol hoists the trash bag back up. "Well, off to the grocery store."

"Why don't I carry that trash down for you," Herbert offers.

"I'd much appreciate that. Thank you, Herb."

"Did you know Ms. Rosa has a dog?" Herbert asks as they make their way toward the stairs.

I sigh and head back inside to find Aunt Paula trying to sit down in her recliner, but I don't reach her in time, and she flops down, sending her crutches flying, nearly missing her injured ankle.

"Aunt Paula!"

She glances up at me. "What?"

"Why didn't you wait for help?"

"Because I can do this on my own. Besides, you'll be working, and I'll need to manage when you're not here. Might as well start now."

"I'll be here as much as possible. I'm only leaving for meetings. Now"—I pick up her crutches and rest them against the wall—"what shall we have for breakfast?"

"I looked. Everything I want requires me to stand."

"I'm cooking. How about oatmeal?"

Aunt Paula makes a face. "No."

"How about a nice egg scramble? I can throw in some extra protein. A little sausage or bacon?" I peer around the kitchen wall, and I'm hit with nostalgia. Uncle Andrew used to chase me around and around the pass-through kitchen, and Aunt Paula would have a fit, saying we were going to hurt ourselves and to take it outside. Poor Uncle Andrew, I think about her cheating and swallow hard over a lump forming in my throat.

"That's too much work." Aunt Paula waves her hand at me.

"Well, we must eat. If you don't tell me exactly what you want, I'll put lima beans in your egg scramble." I cross my arms, standing in front of the peninsula.

"You're just like your mother, you know that? Always with the snarky attitude."

I try to think of a witty reply, but I'm suddenly very warm, as though I'm running a fever. "Is it hot in here?"

Aunt Paula looks up at the fan. "I guess it feels a little warmer than usual. What's the thermostat set at?"

I move toward the unit on the wall and check it. "It says 83. I thought it was set at 80?"

"It should be. Is there cold air coming from the vents?"

I grab the step stool from the pantry closet, move it to the nearest vent, and put my hand in front of it. A wash of nauseated fear comes over me as I climb back down. "It's blowing hot air."

"Darn, it looks like the AC unit is broken."

The room spins as anxiety creeps up, feeding into my voice. "Broken?" I croak.

# CHAPTER 8

"What do you mean, you'll handle it *after* your shift?" I stomp after Aaron and Ransom as they make their way to a black-and-white SUV with the Glendale Police logo across it. The dog looks back at me with a goofy crooked-teeth smile, and it feels like his eyes are focused not just on my eyes, but deeper. As though he wants to know about my feelings by reading my soul. He has these little Croc-like shoes on his paws, and if I wasn't so stressed, I'd take a picture to remember the adorableness of it.

"Sorry, I don't know how my mom handles these things. She probably uses a specific company to service the units."

"Shouldn't that be in a manual or a handbook she gave you before she left?" I throw my hands out. "Have you checked the coffee table?"

"The coffee table?"

The sun's reflection off Aaron's dark-shaded sunglasses prevents me from seeing what his eyes are doing.

"It's a lower version of a kitchen table." I show him with my hands. "Usually used to store random documents, folded laundry, empty ice cream bowls." I throw my hands wide in frustration. "Coasters!"

"Ah, the coaster holder. No." He grins. "I'll try to reach her and see what I can do."

"You can't leave someone without air conditioning. It's some sort of apartment law or something."

"Title 33-1663. Ten days to fix it, and I'm late for work. You're welcome to call your own people and see if they can come out, but I can't guarantee my mom will cover it."

"Ten days! You're a cop. Don't you have some sort of authority or power . . . or . . . badge? Show them your badge." I shove my hands on my hips and take a deep breath, but the air is so thick with heat it causes me to gasp as my throat goes dry.

"Look, why don't *you* and your aunt stay with a neighbor until we can get it sorted out?"

"Because I have to work."

"Oh, like me. Are you late for your job today as well?" He loads Ransom into the back and then climbs into the driver's seat.

"You could be a little nicer right now. Anyway, please just . . ." The heat is making me weak.

"Look." He grips the steering wheel and turns his head. "I didn't break the AC unit, and I can't fix it. All I can do is find out what my mom would do. Give me your number, and I'll get back to you." He pulls out his cell phone.

By accident, I ramble off my work number instead of my personal cell. But I don't correct myself once I notice I've made the mistake. As I watch him back out of the parking spot and onto the main road, I grumble, "Grumpy cop!"

I continue to stand in the parking lot, trying to cool down my anger. If we all weren't rushing from place to place, maybe we would be nicer, better people. But that's what it feels like we've become, rushing from place to place only to hurry off to the next thing. Even in Sun City, where no one should be in a hurry, they are.

"Is everything alright?" a tall man says, pushing his key into the metal mailbox.

I step back towards the open Palms Place gate and enter the arch. "I'm sorry, I forgot your name."

"Apartment 9, George."

"Yes." I shake my head, oddly surprised he doesn't have his hand wrapped around a beer koozie. "George, well, not really. My aunt's air conditioning unit seems to be broken; it's blowing hot air."

"That's horrible, but if it's blowing, that probably means your Freon is low. Technically, not broken. Would you like to stay at my place until Maria—oh, that's right, *Aaron*—gets it fixed? I see he's left you a bit rattled." He removes the mail from the box and locks it back up.

"Thank you. That is such a relief." I follow him back through to the courtyard. "I need to fix her breakfast first, then we'll be over."

"Nonsense. I can cook just as well as the next person. Maybe not Herbert, but pretty darn close. My late wife taught me."

"That's asking too much." I wave him off as we head up the stairs.

"I'm not making Thanksgiving dinner, just breakfast." He smiles and turns left while I go right. "See you in a minute."

"Aunt Paula." I step into the living room. "George has offered for us to stay his place while we straighten out the AC unit."

"That is so kind of him. I hate to put him out." She scoots forward on the recliner.

"George thinks it's just Freon. Aaron was zero help, and I was so flustered I gave him my work number. Crap, work. I need to get logged on."

"Oh, Kel, I think this is just too much. It seems like such a headache for you."

"I'd like to focus on one thing at a time. Then we can worry about the rest. Now, come on, George is offering to make us breakfast."

"I haven't spent a lot of time with George yet, so maybe the air conditioner going out is a gift; a chance for us to get to know each other better."

I count to three and hoist her up, placing the crutches under her. "And when we get back, we can get you showered."

"Maybe."

I'm familiar with avoidance, so if she thinks she can give me the runaround, she's going to have to try harder. I see the fear often from people with a history of falls. Something as simple as stepping in and out of the shower to keep yourself clean seems like you're stepping out of a plane thirty thousand feet in the air.

I gather up my work laptop, cell phone, notepad, and purse, then lock up Aunt Paula's apartment as we head over to George's. We're three feet from his apartment when the shriek of a fire alarm goes off inside. The front door flies open. George and a cloud of smoke escape onto the terrace next to us.

"Small fire. All good now. Little smoky." He waves a dish towel at the door as we stand there in the morning heat. "Little smoky."

# CHAPTER 9

Our invitation to George's went up in smoke, literally. However, Herbert was nice enough to invite Aunt Paula, myself, and George over for a chef's-style brunch. The walls around Herbert's apartment hold medals and photos of all things military, causing me to feel like I'm in one of those old army movies my dad used to watch. There is a Marine Corp flag on one wall, and the tan paint blends with the golden frames. He has a historic cathode ray tube TV with rabbit ears on the top. Everything is outdated but spotless. A stack of magazines and coasters sits on the coffee table. The lamp shade mutes the harshness, casting a '70s brownish-yellow hue around the room. With the blinds closed to keep out the heat, darkness looms in the corners. The light over the table hangs by a chain that would be more suited for a playground swing. The kind where if you aren't careful, the skin on your palm gets pinched and leaves rust marks on rainy days.

"Thank you so much for such a wonderful meal." Aunt Paula checks her leather strap watch, leaning back in Herbert's dining room chair.

"Thanks, Herb," George mumbles, embarrassment still deeply etched on his face.

"It was my pleasure. I'm used to cooking for groups of people. Back in the Marines, I did it all, from flipping flapjacks to roasting potatoes." Herbert takes a long sip from his coffee mug that he has refilled twice since we gathered around his dining room table.

"Didn't mean to put you out like this," George mentions, wiping his handlebar mustache with his napkin. "I owe you."

There is a various mix of fast-food restaurant napkins in a pile on the table.

"I'll take you up on that. I need to get the oil changed in my truck, and my back is tweaked a bit, could use some help underneath, if you're able." Herbert sets the mug on the table and rests his elbows on the worn wood.

"Just let me know when, and I'll grab my overalls." George gives a tilt of his head.

"Yes, thank you." I push out my chair and stand. "I hate to eat and run to work, but I'm already late." My work cell phone chimes and I realize I've missed a call, but there's a voicemail. "Excuse me."

I close Herbert's front door behind me, and I exit onto the terrace overlooking the courtyard as the phone rings again. "Sharon's Angels, this is Kelly."

"Yes, I need help, and no one has called me," the voice says.

"I'm sorry. Who is this?"

"Mary Venable. You're supposed to do my medical."

"Yes, sorry. I'm not currently in front of my computer. Can I take your number just in case and call you back in a bit?"

"But I need help. I've been waiting for weeks."

"I'm sorry, Mary. The caseloads are a little high right now." A beep interrupts my words, and I pull it away from my ear to see an incoming call.

"When can you come out to see me?"

"If you're having a health emergency, you can go to urgent care." I've come to learn that people's definition of emergency is broad. As are the terms *sometimes* and *once in a while.*

"I don't need to see a doctor. I need help." Mary raises her voice. "Do I need to be dying to get help?"

I take a deep breath. "I didn't say that, Mary. I just need to look at my calendar to determine when I can get your evaluation done."

"Fine," Mary huffs. "Whatever." Then the line goes dead.

I pull the phone away from my ear to see she's hung up, and I now have two voicemails. The problem is, I don't know if Mary is from my regular caseload or if she's one of the clients I'm supposed to see on my temporary list down here.

"Everything alright, Kelly?"

I spin around and find Rosa behind me. "Hi, yeah, just another day at work."

"Don't you work too hard. You need to do the relaxing." Rosa threads her hands around the strap of her flamingo-pink purse, and she takes a puff from her cigarette. "Have you seen the police?"

"Aaron, the cop? He's at work. But my aunt's air-conditioning went out, so I've been waiting for his call. Do you know who usually comes out to fix this sort of thing?"

Rosa raises an eye as though the answer is on her eyelash. "No remember."

A cell phone rings like an old-school home phone, letting me know it's my personal cell and not work. It's so hot out that I'm sweating through both my tank tops and shorts. *Dry heat, my a—*

"Rosa! Rosa!"

I glance over the railing to see a familiar head of hair moving around the courtyard on his way to the stairs.

Rosa spots the man, too, and leans over the railing.

"I saw it." Fred takes the steps off balance but two at a time. My body tenses, watching him, as I envision him toppling down the stairs.

Rosa hurries off past me, taking the long way around the terrace, away from Fred. He's on the last step now.

"You saw no things!" Rosa shouts.

I bring my hand to my forehead and clamp my eyes shut. When I open them back up, Fred speed-walks past me, and I welcome the breeze he stirs up. Rosa's wedge sandals clomp on the concrete, echoing through the area. It's like watching the couple in a cuckoo clock chase each other at noon.

"You come back here and admit what I saw!" Fred raises his fist.

Rosa grabs the handrail and scurries down the stairs. Fred is gaining ground and hurries towards the stairs.

I wonder if I should intervene when Rosa stops and spins around. Fred slams into her. I run down the stairs and prepare myself to break up an elderly fight. *Wait, is that even a thing?* As I approach, their height difference is noticeable to the point of being humorous. Rosa could never have outrun Fred; he is at least four feet taller than her, and her three steps were no match for his one.

"You. Saw. No. Things." Rosa's glaring at Fred, and he's straining his neck, looking down.

"You have a—"

"Temporary." Rosa's hand reaches up and covers his mouth. "It could've been dead if I'd not saved it."

*The dog. Fred knows about the dog.*

"Dead?" Fred mumbles through her cupped hand.

Rosa lowers her hand back down to her side. "Yes, bad person left it in a hot car."

"Why didn't you say that?"

"Sometimes Fred . . ." Rosa glances at me, then back to Fred. "Sometimes you forget what people say."

"Oh." Fred frowns, and his eyes travel to his flip-flops. "I see."

"Come on, Fred, you want to meet the"—Rosa glances around and whispers—"dog?"

Fred thinks about it, running his hand through his short gray mass of hair that could belong to Sam Elliot. "I guess, if you trust me."

Rosa links her arm into the crook of his. "Of course, Fred, of course."

I watch them make their way toward Rosa's apartment. Then I pull out my personal cell and see I missed a call from Drew. I tap the voicemail icon and put the phone to my ear.

"Hi, Kelly, it's Drew. I guess it's a good thing you're spending more time with your aunt. Anyway, I hope this means you get time off work, because well, you never take time off. Anyway, sorry, I'm rambling. Just be safe. It's a lot different down there than up here. So, anyway. Okay, bye."

I sigh and gently bite my lower lip. No *I love you*. No *I miss you*. I close my eyes and see him and that woman. And my mind imagines the things they did together because I don't believe they only talked. I can't shake the thought, and I worry I never will be able to.

# CHAPTER 10

Thankfully, one voicemail was from Aaron letting me know he reached his mom, and the technician would be out in the next four hours. The other voicemail is work related.

I instantly regret returning to my aunt's sweltering apartment as I try to get work done. The only place I have privacy to work with cool air is my car. George offered to take my aunt to the movies so I could work alone in his apartment, but it still smelled of burned sausages. It's hard to air out a place when you can't open the windows or doors because it's 108 outside.

I hold my work cell phone to my ear as it rings on the other side. Someone picks up the line with a grumble.

"Mary, it's Kelly from Sharon's Angels. I'm finally at my computer and see you're on Reems Road in Surprise?"

"Yes." Mary coughs into the phone.

"Great, I can come out to see you tomorrow at either ten in the morning or three in the afternoon." I already scheduled four other meetings for the day, but they're all at the same rehab center, so at least I won't be driving all over the place.

"I have a doctor's appointment at nine thirty, so I guess we can do three. But I'll be tired by then. Maybe we can meet before my appointment?"

"I'm sorry, but I'm booked for the day."

"Fine. Three." Mary hangs up without a goodbye, and I shake my head, slamming my phone on the table. *Rude!*

The ice in my glass of water has melted and is now luke-warm. I take a sip anyway and replay the words of Drew's voicemail in my head.

"Chocolate. I need chocolate." I head to the refrigerator and fling open the door. I spot a bag of chocolate-covered almonds in a butter dish and carry it back to the table.

With the internet tab open, I log into our portal and check the internal job board for listings. They're still accepting resumes for the supervisor position. I've opened and re-read the job description a handful of times since it was posted three weeks ago. My manager even messaged me to apply, stating I'd be great for it. And I could really use the increase in pay.

Sweat drips across my forehead, and I check the time in the corner of my laptop, still another three hours to go in the window of time for the repairman to show up.

I look at the salary listed for supervisor and grab another handful of chocolate; they melt in my hand. My work phone rings, and I pick it up, smearing the chocolate from my hand across it. I groan. "Sharon's Angel, this is Kelly."

Putting the call on speaker, I head to the kitchen to grab a paper towel to clean my phone and hand.

"Yes, Kelly, it's Mark Swanson, you did an evaluation on my mother two weeks ago. Well, we got the letter that she wasn't eligible for the program."

"Hi, Mark, yes," I think of who he's calling about. I've seen at least twenty people since I did his mom's initial evaluation, but I knew he wasn't going to be happy with the outcome.

"How do you sleep at night?" Mark asks.

I wipe off the cell and take him off speaker. "Excuse me?"

"You're denying people that need help. How do you sleep at night knowing you're putting people at risk?"

I try my best to take a deep breath and slow my increasing heart rate. My blood pressure is surely spiking as I shake a little. It happens every time someone is upset with me. Even after all these years, I can't seem to keep my nerves from being rattled. "I'm sorry she wasn't eligible. However, I don't make the criteria for our program. It's the same for everyone. If you'd like, we can go over why she didn't qualify?"

"You better hope she doesn't die, because that's on *you* now," Mark barks and the call ends.

I fall into the dining room chair and toss my phone on the table. I'm so over this. I'm over the nasty calls, the ungrateful people. My eyes stare blankly at the laptop screen. I want out. But what if I get the supervisor spot and fail? I've read through the requirements, and I can put a check next to all of them. Yet, I've heard through the grapevine that the head supervisor over the position is a real piece of work.

My hand hovers over the mouse pad. My current position has its perks, along with a great boss . . . I know everything I'm doing, I'm comfortable, and I know what's expected of me. I think about all the times I've been treated kindly at meetings. The list is short and allows me to flip easily through the memories. The one that stands out the most was an invitation to stay with the daughter of a client who lived in London. If I was ever in town, just give her a jingle on her *mobile* phone, and she'd make sure I had a delightful time. While we could never take anyone up on any offer or accept gifts, the thought always counted.

Once I had to toss out a yummy-looking chocolate cake from the Cheesecake Factory because the client's family had delivered it to our main office address. I'd never seen so many sad staff faces. If it'd arrived at my front door, I would've had it for dinner.

I move the cursor to the corner of the screen and my finger hovers with the arrow over the X. Then I think about Mary and Mark's phone call, and it's not even noon yet. I move the mouse back to the left of the screen and click the apply button instead.

There's a loud knock at the door. My shirt is stuck to my back, and I yank it away from my skin as I make my way to open it.

"Hi, I'm here to fix the AC." The man is dressed in blue overalls, and his skin is as tan as a burned loaf of cracked wheat sourdough bread.

"Thank goodness!" I want to hug him but shoot my hands up in the air instead as though I won the jackpot on *The Price is Right*. "Do you need to come inside?"

He walks in and places his hand on the vent. "It's blowing air, just not cold." He clicks off the thermostat.

"Thanks."

"You're probably just low on Freon." He grabs the brim of his hat, nods, and heads outside.

I shut the door. Not that the temperature feels much different between the two anymore and make my way to the thermostat. It reads 93, and my eyes nearly burst from their sockets. "Dear goodness."

Without locking up, I head over to Herbert's and give the door a gentle knock.

He opens it with a smile. "Why Ms. Kelly, I'd be lying if I said that Ms. Paula's air-conditioning has put me out. It's been a delight to get to chat with her."

I cup my hands together and bring them to my chin. "That's good to hear." Then I raise my voice a little. "She always drives me nuts."

"I can hear you," Aunt Paula chimes from the couch, and we laugh.

"Great news, the AC tech is here, and he thinks it's just the Freon." My shoulders relax as I step inside, and Herbert closes the door. The cold air hits my sweat-covered body, and it's such a relief. I'm also beyond the acceptable standards of hygiene and must take a shower as soon as possible. There is no way I smell good.

"Aunt Paula, it's over 90 degrees in there, so even if he fixes it, it'll take hours for it to cool back down to 80."

"True." Herbert opens the refrigerator and grabs a jug of what looks like iced tea. "Can I offer you some?"

"Thank you, but I have to get back to work. I just wanted to come over and give you an update."

"At least take it to go." Herbert pours the liquid into a glass and hands it to me.

"I appreciate it. I'll bring the glass back." I pivot to turn and catch myself in déjà vu, perhaps in a prior life I lived in Palms Place, each apartment feeling more familiar than the last. I glance back at Herbert taking a seat on the sofa next to Aunt Paula. Giving them a smile, I step outside. Hebert might be a rule following ex-Marine, but deep down inside he seems like a caring person, and highly misunderstood.

"I saw the van in the parking lot!" Carol calls up from the pool.

"Yes." I take a sip of iced tea and wrap my free hand around the railing. "Should be fixed soon."

"If you have time, come and join me for a dip. I dropped five bags of ice in here, so it's nice and refreshing."

"Thanks, but I have to get back to work." I raise the glass to her and head back inside my aunt's apartment.

Returning to my makeshift workstation, I lower myself onto the chair and set the sweaty glass on the table. Blindly, I reach into the bowl of chocolate and my fingers are instantly coated in melted chocolate.

"Oh, gosh!" I take the chocolate and drop it in the trash and head towards the sink when a knock comes at the door. "Come in!"

I can't see who's there as I finish washing my hands and grab the dish towel on the stove's handle. "Fixed already?"

But when I come around the corner, Aaron and Ransom are standing in the living room wearing their police attire.

"Oh, I thought you were the electrician."

"Well, Ransom can be pretty shocking." He glances at the K-9.

"Shockingly handsome." I smile at the dog and realize how much I miss Joey back home.

"I just wanted to swing by and see if everything was taken care of." He held Ransom's leash loosely, and the dog moved into a relaxed sit, his back legs splaying into the shape of a V.

"Yes, he's up there right now. Oh, did you see Rosa yet? She needed help with her sink." I continue wiping my hands with the dish towel even though they're dry.

Ransom's tongue hangs sideways out of his mouth, and he stands, stretching his big bearlike paws forward and flops on his belly.

"Long day already?" I point at the dog.

"Yes, we had a situation at a house, had to send him in, he'll sleep good tonight."

"Can I ask you about his name?"

"Ransom? It felt fitting for a K-9."

I bite my lip, feeling silly about the question now. "It really does."

"I actually came by to apologize for this morning." Aaron looks uncomfortable, his eyes unfocused. He glances at me, then around the room.

I wave my hand at him. "No need. I was stressed and didn't know what to do. The AC not working in the middle of summer is worrisome for me. I should have approached you differently."

"No, I'm here to help my mom out, and I woke up on the wrong side of the bed. My ex-wife and I were on the phone late . . . it was a long night; I didn't get much sleep."

With work, I'm constantly put in the middle of family disagreements, such as who will take care of mom or dad. I avoid arguments and misunderstandings as much as possible, but this felt different, as though Aaron is someone I can connect with about what I'm going through.

"I'm sorry to hear that." I don't know him, and he doesn't know me, so does my concern matter? "I bet having Ransom by your side is great. I wish I had a buddy that went everywhere with me. We have a dog, Joey, but it's really my husband's dog."

Aaron frowns and squats down, rubbing the top of Ransom's head. The dog's eyes go up toward the ceiling in delight of the affection. "Yes, he's a great buddy, but he punches me in his sleep."

I laugh and kneel at the K-9's level, giving him pets, too. His fur is soft, especially his ear. "You let him sleep in your bed?"

"He sort of insists. But he has some wild dreams. He'll snort and do this bubbler thing with his lips. I laugh every time. Then his paws get going and there is no stopping where they land." He gives Ransom a few more strokes on the head.

I'm still kneeling, but stop petting him, and I just stare at how cute I find Ransom and his soul-seeking eyes.

"*Sitzen*." Aaron instructs as the K-9 sits. "Ransom, this is Kelly. Can you shake?"

Ransom lifts his left paw, and I instantly laugh. I reach my hand out and take his bear-like paw for a few seconds before letting go. Then Ransom springs forward and licks my face. I stumble backwards and land on my bottom. But I'm laughing hard and so is Aaron. I squint through my dog-slobbered eyelashes and see Aaron's hand coming toward me. I take it as he lifts me back up to my feet.

"Sorry, gosh, he doesn't seem to have any manners around you, either." Aaron grips the leash as Ransom's tail smacks the side of the coffee table over and over.

"Trust me, I need a bath. He was only helping me get a head start."

Behind Aaron, there is a knock on the open front door, and when I stand, Rosa is there.

"Aaron, my sink is full of leaks." Rosa blows a puff of cigarette smoke over the side of her shoulder. "I'm running out of buckets."

"Sure, I have a quick minute or two." Aaron scratches the back of his head, and I notice his body slump. "I'll see you around."

As he steps outside with Ransom, I say, "Yeah, see you."

But as they walk away, I notice my heart is racing. I know it's wrong; I'm still married. I'm not an eye-for-an-eye type of person. And that's when it hits me. Truth deep inside my heart—I know Drew slept with that woman. It's the only reason why I look at men differently now, because doubt is laced around my wedding ring, and it hurts to look at it. I can't continue to be so naïve. I shut the door and spin around, sliding down it to the carpet below and cr y.

# CHAPTER 11

"My eyeballs are floating!" Aunt Paula bursts through her apartment door using her left crutch to kick the door open. She scurries towards the bathroom like a mouse running from a cat. I watch her nearly stumble as she drops the crutches and tries to shut the door with them in the way.

I pick them up as the door latches. "Why didn't you use Herbert's restroom?"

But she doesn't respond. After setting the crutches against the wall, I stand under the blowing air vent in the hall. She finally emerges, leaning on the doorknob and counter.

"Well?" I hand her one crutch at a time.

"I can't go at his place. He doesn't have grab bars, and I was not asking him for help off his toilet."

"Why didn't you just come back here to go?"

"So, he knew I was going potty?" Her jaw hangs open as though it's detached from her face.

"Yes, I think Herbert is aware of how the body functions. He's the one serving us glasses of iced tea." I shake my head. "Turn back around. Let's get you showered, then we can focus on dinner."

Aunt Paula glances behind me and then moves to the living room. "No, I'll do that later."

"No. You didn't even finish the shower when you fell." I point at the bathroom. "You owe me a shower and a half."

"Let's have supper first. I'm starving. I think we have something we can throw together."

A knock at the door derails my plans for trying to drag her into the bathroom. Aunt Paula flops into her recliner as I hurry past.

"*Bonsoir*, Kelly." Vivian peers around me at the front door. "And a good evening to you, Paula." She holds a decorative glass bowl with both hands. And I notice she has on a name tag sticker with Vivian perfectly inked across it.

"Please come in." I step back and she comes inside. "Why are you wearing a name tag? Bingo night at the community center?"

"No, that's on Wednesday. The residents all got together and figured it would be much easier for you if you didn't have to worry about remembering our names."

"Thank you, but I think I'm doing okay remembering."

Vivian tilts her head toward Aunt Paula as though to check if I'm indeed correct. "I whipped up a BVS for you. I didn't think either of you were in the mood to make dinner, with the AC issue and all."

"BVS?" I run my tongue over the front of my teeth as though the meaning is hidden like broccoli between my eye tooth and lateral incisor.

"Big Vivian Salad." Vivian lifts the bowl towards me.

I take it with a laugh. "Thanks."

"Yes, thank you, Vivian." Aunt Paula waves the remote control at her. "Want to join us?"

"No, I'll leave you to it. *Au revoir*." Vivian does a side head nod and is out the door like a breeze.

I lock it behind her and take the BVS to the kitchen's peninsula and remove the lid. The smell of olives, onions, grilled chicken, tomatoes, and goat cheese fills my nose. It's like a painting for the senses. Everything appears perfectly sliced as a mixed-up rainbow. "You have dressing, right?"

"Yes, several in the refrigerator door, and there are some pita crackers in the cupboard we can have with it."

I hear the *I Love Lucy* theme song on the living room TV as I find everything we need and prepare our plates. Once I have my aunt's plate, I grab two of the salad dressings and make my way to the living room.

"Which one?" I hand her the plate and wiggle the options.

"Italian." She reaches for it.

I watch as she slathers on more than I would yet is careful to miss the pita chips resting on the side. "I need to finish up a few things with work. Do you mind if I eat at the table?"

"It's after five."

"I know, but I fell behind with everything going on today. I just wanted to check on a few cases."

She gives me a side-eye of disapproval. "If you must."

I must. I always must. Because that's how my job works. Stay on top of things so that the snowball doesn't grow any bigger. Although it's already too big and is rolling down the massive mountain with my coworkers and I imbedded in it.

I load my plate and choose to make my dressing—a little olive oil, salt, and pepper. "Oh, do you want something to drink?"

"Just some iced tea if you don't mind," she says over the crowd's laughter at Lucy's antics.

I drop ice cubes into the glasses and fill them to the top with tea, listening to the ice in the glasses pop and crack.

"Here you go." I set her glass on the end table and take mine to the dining room table.

Wiggling my middle finger on the mouse pad, my laptop screen comes on. It blinks and I allow it to refresh while taking a few stabs at my salad. "This is delicious." I shove another bite into my mouth. "Far better than a premade one from the grocery store."

"I'm a big fan of the BVS." Aunt Paula holds up her fork when I turn around in my chair.

"It might need another name. It sounds like a disease or a summer Bible camp."

"Vivian can call it whatever she wants. I've had about six of her meals and she can make an egg in a shoe taste good."

"Why are you eating shoes? Are your social security checks *that* bad?"

She laughs and I don't know if it's at my lame joke or Lucy and Ricky. I click around on my laptop and take a long sip of iced tea. The air-conditioning is working hard to make it back to 80 as the noise covers the apartment. I click open the program where our caseload data is held. I choke, trying hard to control the tea from spraying all over my laptop screen. My number of cases displayed on the main page is 103. *One hundred! And three!*

"Everything okay, Kel?"

I hear my aunt's voice, but it sounds like it's miles away as the blood fills my eardrums. Sure, we have high caseloads, but this is insane. Triple digits always cause panic, no matter what it is—the summer weather temperatures, mortgages, and bills, and for me, caseload sizes. Unless you're a jackpot winner, triple digits can take a hike.

I move the cursor over the number and click, allowing me to see the individual cases, and reassure myself that the number is high because my supervisor added the Maricopa County cases but forgot to remove the Coconino County ones. However, as I organize them by zip code, to my dismay, I see that I no longer have any Flag zip codes.

I scroll so fast my pointer finger cramps up, hoping that I just need to go far enough down on the list to find my older cases. But there is not a single one. I check the time in the screen's corner. I'm hiding the fact that I'm on after hours by turning my chat status to Away, which means I can't email or call my supervisor to find out what is happening with my caseload. Instead, I draft an email to her and schedule it to send five minutes after my start time tomorrow morning so I can focus on more pressing matters when I log on.

Leaning into the chair, I take a few bites of salad and find it hard to swallow. I'm too stressed to keep eating the best salad I've ever had in my life. Then I add fuel to my internal fire and look at the due dates of the cases. At least four are already overdue and another chunk is due this week. *How is that possible?*

"You can't stress about what you can't control." Aunt Paula mutes the TV, and, minus the low hum of the air-conditioning, the apartment is quiet.

I spin around in the chair and lay my right arm over the back of it. "I can't *not* stress about it."

"And why not?"

I open my mouth to respond, but my retired teacher aunt has a long history of skilled negations and tactics to wrangle entire groups of children. Excuses bounce off her like a child on a trampoline, so I know I must think before I answer.

At the end of a deep breath I say, "Because"—*don't start with because, that's Excuse 101*—"you see, my job requires me to be timely and to provide quality. Therefore, we must do the impossible. Even though quality and quantity don't mix."

I sit up straight, waiting her response. But her face is not giving away how she feels. We stare at each other for what feels like minutes.

"That must be stressful." Aunt Paula rests her fork on the plate.

"It is, and Drew is always saying that my entire life revolves around my work, and I can see that. I'm not oblivious to it. And while I want to get fired, I can't afford it, so I do whatever I have to do to make sure I'm never on management's radar."

"You've been in this position for over ten years. Do you think you can do it for another ten? Can you do it without having a nervous breakdown? Maybe it's time to explore other roles within the company or, perhaps, elsewhere?"

"Some days I sure feel like I'm about to break, but change makes me nervous and stressed, and I have enough of it going on already. I don't need to add more."

"Do you think that's why Drew . . . was spending time with the other woman?"

The words hit my ears, and they sound gross. *The other woman.* I make my way to the edge of the couch and sit down, facing her. "Why did you cheat on Uncle Andrew?"

Aunt Paula bites her bottom lip. "All marriages have rough patches. I take full responsibility for what happened, not that it makes it right. Andrew and I were struggling with communicating, and we were having a few issues. Instead of seeking help, I began spending time with another teacher after school." She sets her fork down and stares at her plate. "That was when I learned good people can make mistakes. Don't get me wrong, you have a right to the truth, as well as to be angry, hurt, and upset. The question you need to ask yourself is can you forgive Drew and can you forget? See, Kelly, sometimes, no matter how much we forgive someone, if we can't forget, then forgiving may not be enough to get past."

# CHAPTER 12

I think it's the alarm on my cell going off, but when I sit up on the couch; I realize it's the doorbell. Since I've arrived, everyone who has come to the door has knocked, so I'm not even aware there was a doorbell. I swing my legs over the couch and blink the sleep from my eyes. Light is coming through the living room curtains, which means it's at least five thirty in the morning.

With a groan, I stand, spotting Aunt Paula in the recliner. My left knee pops as I make my way to the front door. I've been sleeping in her bed since she can't get comfortable in it. The spare room is still full of moving boxes, but we watched a movie last night, and I never made it off the couch.

Fatigue courses through me as though I didn't get any sleep at all. I open the door without checking to see who is on the other side. My eyes widen when I notice the police officer uniform and a dog.

"Morning."

I gaze at him, still half asleep, and realize I know this cop and this dog. *Grumpy Cop.* "Aaron, good morning. And"—I look down—"Ransom, good morning."

Ransom greets me by giving my pants a sniff.

"I wanted to make sure the air conditioner was running, okay?" Aaron doesn't smile. His lips are straight, as though undecided what mood he is in this early in the day.

"Oh, yes." I lean on the door frame and cross my arms, realizing I don't have a bra on. "It finally cooled down to normal sometime late last night."

I see Carol walking on the other side of the terrace. She's wearing neon orange leggings and a turquoise tank top. Aaron catches my gaze and looks behind him as she speed walks around the corner, heading straight for us.

"*Bleiben*," Aaron instructs as Ransom freezes.

"Good morning. Good morning," Carol hums as she speeds past. "Getting my steps in while there is still shade to be had!"

We watch as she hurries down the stairs and makes her next loop around the lower courtyard. Aaron turns back to me.

"Thank you for your follow-up about the air conditioning. We appreciate it."

"Rumor has it you're staying around for a while to help your aunt out?"

"Yes, for at least a few weeks." I nod. "I'm working remotely."

"What is it you do?" Aaron asks.

"I'm a social worker, specializing in the medical field."

"A nurse?"

"No, I couldn't handle that level of medical-ness. Just a social worker." I feel the disappointment cross over my face. It's such an undesirable and unappealing job to bother to mention. It's not a boastful career like a lawyer or a doctor. Nor is it honorable, like a cop or a farmer. It's the type of job that when you tell someone they tilt their head, g o *aww*, and mention how hard it must be, but they're just happy they aren't you.

"That's a challenging job," Aaron says.

"So I've heard." I huff a laugh. "I've worked with a few local law enforcement officers up in Flagstaff when things have gotten out of hand. Do you come across that a lot here?"

"There is some off-and-on work with CPS. We work more with APS and detectives or active crime scenes. Ransom works as a scent dog."

"For explosives, drugs?"

"No, mostly search and rescue, man trailing. But he's not a cadaver dog."

I stand there, my mouth agape. "I thought that was a German shepherd thing or a bloodhound?"

"All depends on the dog, but Labs are among the top breeds used."

"Fascinating. Sorry, I should let you get going."

"Right." He runs his hand through his short hair. "Anyway, I just wanted to double check that the AC was okay."

I continue to lean on the door. "Thank you. Were you able to fix Rosa's sink?"

"Yes, it took a few trips to Ace, but it's done now. Well . . ." Aaron directs Ransom's leash forward with his hand, says, "Kommen," and the dog pivots toward the stairs. "Have a nice day."

"Thanks, stay safe." I watch Carol come back up the steps, looping around again as Aaron and Ransom head down.

I start to close the door when Herbert appears to the right. "Happy Tuesday, Ms. Kelly." He glances at Aaron and Ransom. "I see we're allowing the dog up here now. Fine. Fine."

"It's too early to be hostile, Herbert."

"Only stating a fact, Ms. Kelly. How is your aunt this morning?"

"Well, the fact is, Ransom, is a police officer." I mumble and step outside because if Aunt Paula didn't want to use Herbert's restroom, she surely wouldn't want him to see her half asleep in the recliner in her pajamas.

"She's well." I close the door behind me. "It's already very warm out."

"Currently, it's only 95. The forecast is for 118. Be sure you drink lots of water." He adjusts his Vietnam Veterans hat. "Will you need me to check in on your aunt today? She mentioned you were working."

"Oh, she should be fine. I'll be in and out all day." I bite my lower lip just thinking about how much I must accomplish today.

"I see." Herbert's vision shifts down to his spotless tennis shoes.

"However, she might want some company. Maybe a game of cards or to watch a movie."

"I shall keep that in mind, although I doubt she'd want to hang out with me two days in a row. Have a good day, Ms. Kelly." He tips the brim of his black hat and heads back inside his apartment.

"Don't you be getting any ideas," Aunt Paula warns me as I close her front door.

"I'm not. He just seemed so disappointed that you didn't need his assistance today."

She scoots to the edge of the recliner and reaches for her crutches that are leaning up against the wall. I hurry over to grab them for her, but she shoos me away. "I can get them."

"I know you can, but I'm here to help."

"You can help by making us coffee." She wobbles but manages to get the crutches in place, then heads toward the hall.

"How about before I log on, we get you in the shower?"

"It'll be a long hot day. Maybe later tonight, before bed."

"Okay." I check the thermostat to make sure the air conditioning is still holding at 80 degrees. Thankfully, it is. I don't need the added stress. In the kitchen, I prepare the coffee and grab a mug from the cupboard above the maker. Then I grab a glass for myself because I'm putting ice in mine and making it iced coffee.

While it's brewing, I open the refrigerator and realize we're out of coffee creamer. "Dang."

"What's wrong?" Aunt Paula startles me, and I nearly bump my head on the freezer door's handle protruding over my head. It's a retro refrigerator that has its pluses—it looks adorable—and minuses—such as pinching your finger in the handle and bumping your head. "No creamer. I forgot to get some when I was at the store."

"We can ask a neighbor." She leans on her crutch so she can pat my shoulder.

"Like knock on their door and ask to borrow used creamer?"

"Used? It's not regurgitated creamer."

My eyes lace with suspicion. "Fine, I'll go ask . . ." I pause, realizing I'm still in my pajamas and braless. "Who should I ask *after* I get dressed?"

"I'll go ask, you just get ready for work."

"You can't be hobbling around. You should be resting. Plus, there is a high probability of Carol running you over—she's a neon blur."

Aunt Paula's face looks solemn. "I miss our daily walks. She invited me to join her on my first morning here, and I was hooked. We had such fun."

I squeeze her arm. "You'll go again soon. PT starts next week."

But I could see she wasn't sure about how soon it would be. I watch her totter to the front door, then she stops. She's always been an independent woman, even when she was married. Aunt Paula doesn't want to look helpless. There is hesitancy in her steps, and witnessing her fear tugs at my heart.

"Aunt Paula, how about I go? It's too hot." I come up behind her and rest my hand on her back.

Defeat spreads across her face as I walk with her back to the recliner, guiding her down under her arm so she doesn't plop, and then go get dressed.

My work has a dress code, but it's not followed by anyone that I've seen. There is no way to monitor it when we work in the field. Unless, of course, a facility calls up our supervisor. It's one perk that I love. I feel uncomfortable in blouses and dress pants, let alone heels. We walk everywhere, and there is no way I'm walking eight thousand steps a day in anything but comfy tennis shoes. Plus, we spend time with nurses who wear Crocs and scrubs. Seems only fair that my coworkers and I can wear a nice T-shirt and jeans. However, a case manager at a rehab facility once ratted out a coworker of mine who'd showed up in pajamas to a meeting. With such a high turnover rate, I really don't care if a coworker wants to wear pajamas or a ball gown.

I'm dressed in jeans, which I'm thinking I'll regret in this heat, but shorts are not going to happen. There is nothing like your bare legs touching an unknown bodily fluid they shouldn't on a client's couch.

I look at myself in my aunt's bedroom mirror. The T-shirt hangs nicely, covering up my no-longer-thirtysomething, I-can-eat-anything stomach. When I step closer, the image becomes like HDTV, and I'm boldly reminded of my age. The lines on my face run vertically across my forehead. And the lines on my neck look like a '90s-style choker necklace. I wonder if I should get back into that trend just to cover it up. I'm not old, but I don't feel young. And I don't feel beautiful anymore. I haven't for years. I'm reminded why Drew doesn't say the things he used to. *Gorgeous, lovely, pretty*. I wouldn't refer to myself with those words anymore, either. Maybe if I'd been one of those timeless beauties, he wouldn't have cheated.

# Chapter 13

I'm lost. Incredibly lost. But after wandering—not walking, walking meant I knew where I was going—around this massive complex trying to find my client's apartment, I'm ready to die from the heat. The map at the entrance was of zero help. First, I pulled my car over and tried to make heads or tails of it. When did people stop putting YOU ARE HERE stickers on maps? But an impatient driver in the car behind me honked, so I parked and walked back over to the map. Second, the oh-so-gentle Arizona sun had cracked and faded the map's plastic to where it could've passed for the backside of a ninety-year-old person.

Currently, it feels like my skin is melting and dripping from me, and the rubber on the bottom of my tennis shoes is sticking to the pavement. Building T is in front of me, apartments 150-155 on the ground level and 250-255 on the second story. I'm looking for Building S, apartment 332. The complex has a mix of two- and three-story buildings, but some of the first-floor units are down a flight of stairs, disappearing below the landscape. However, until I'm right on them, they *all* look like two-story buildings. When I drove in, Building A was the first one, and I assumed Building S would be closer to the other side of the complex. This caused me to loop around the U-shaped parking lot and head in on the opposite side. However, S seems to be missing altogether. I run through the alphabet one more time, just in case the heat has caused me to forget the order of the letters. Nope, *s* comes before *t*, so Building S should be directly to the left of Building T.

I pause and take a breath. Sweat beads everywhere, and my jeans stick to me as though they're made of leather, like Michelle Pfeiffer in her Catwoman catsuit.

"This is impossible," I say aloud, noticing someone exiting their apartment.

My desire to ask this woman where the heck Building S is halts, and I avert my eyes. She's screaming into her phone and swinging what looks like a bra in her free hand, as though she's about to find the person on the other end of the line and strangle them with it.

I move out of her way and follow another path that leads into the middle of the complex. Then, like a glowing star atop a Christmas tree, hiding behind a big Chinese elm, I spot the faded S.

"Finally!" I groan, mumbling a few inappropriate words under my breath, and head towards the exterior stairs.

But I'm lightheaded, and I stumble on a step. I right myself and hope that the client offers me a water bottle when I get there; my water is back in the little cooler I keep in my Nissan.

Composing myself once I reach the landing, I try to look less sweaty by wiping my forehead with the back of my hand. I find 332 and knock on the door. Dead bugs fill the inside track of the windowsill and outside, a sticky substance has dried mid-run down the front door.

"What?" an angry female voice calls out behind the door.

"I'm Kelly from Sharon's Angels," I lean forward and yell back.

"Well, come in then!"

I grab the hot and sticky doorknob. I guess the substance didn't just get on the front of the door.

"Hi," I call out, walking inside, my eyes readjusting to the darkness. Instantly, I'm hit in the face with thick, stale cigarette smoke, and I cough. "I'm Kelly."

"Yeah, I heard ya the first time." The woman is sitting in a lima-bean green recliner, bare scaly feet up, and is smoking like a stack. But it's not until I step two more feet forward, that I notice she has an oxygen tube in her nose and several spare historic metal bottles around her. She's smoking next to her oxygen tanks. *Oh my goodness!*

"I'm allergic, would you mind?" I point at what's left of her cigarette.

She glares at me as though I've asked if I can eat her thirty-dollar sirloin steak. I want to inform her that smoking with the oxygen tank is dangerous, but I don't think she cares.

"How long will this take?" the woman grumbles and snuffs out the cigarette in the ashtray.

"About half an hour." I look around. There is nowhere to sit, not a couch or chairs at the kitchen table. Food-stained mail and knocked-over medication bottles cover the coffee and side table. "So, Shirley, let's start with your doctors and the medications you take."

"Shirley? Who's that? I'm Martha Broadwell."

"Excuse me?"

"Sweetie, my name is Martha."

I glance down at my paper. SHIRLEY MCKENNA, 17927 W. DESERT WILLOW, APT. 332. "Um, you told me to come in?"

"Yeah, I can't keep track of what I've applied for. If it's not the hospital, it's my doctor, applying for this and that. Do you know how many phone calls I get every day? How am I to remember? What is it you offer?"

"I'm in apartment 332, right?"

"Yeppers." Martha crosses her arms. "But ya can go ahead and see if I qualify for your program, since you're here."

I shake my head and check the time on my fitness watch. "I'm sorry, you'll need to apply first. Excuse me for the mistake." I turn and head for the front door but stop and spin back around. "Don't let strangers into your apartment. I could've been anyone."

"You're not a stranger." She picks back up her cigarette. "What company did ya say you were? Do ya have a form to fill out?"

"Sharon's Angels, and no, sorry, I don't have any applications with me. You can call our main line." I pull out a business card and hand it to her. "Or fill one out online."

"I don't have a computer." She flicks a lighter at the squished, half-used cigarette. "Lock the little thing on the knob, would ya?"

I press my lips together, stiffening a groan. I engage the useless lock and walk back out into the heat.

Grabbing the handrail, I make my way down the three flights of stairs and try to back track how I got to Building S. I loop this way and that way, before tripping over a section of sidewalk that has buckled from an Arizona ash tree's roots. I regain my balance and finally spot my car. There is a wavy mirage over the top of it. I unlock it and blast the AC while I locate the number listed for the client who is *not* living in apartment 332 and hit send.

On the third ring, someone answers. "Hello?"

"Hi yes, this is Kelly with Sharon's Angels. May I please speak with Shirley?"

"Speaking."

"Hi, we have a meeting at eleven thirty today. However, I seem to have the wrong address for you."

"You're late."

I glance at the time in my car, 11:42. "Yes, I'm sorry, I went to the address on file, but you don't live in apartment 332 in Building S."

"Uh, 332? No, I live in apartment 233. I get my numbers mixed up from time to time. When will you be here?"

"I'm here, at the apartment complex. What building letter are you in, is it S?"

"I think so. I haven't lived here long, and I never leave my place. How much longer will you be?"

*Do not react. Do. Not. React.* "You provided the incorrect apartment number, Shirley, so just give me a few minutes to find the correct one. Now, when you come into the complex, do you go right or left?"

"Right."

"Okay, and are you further in the back or off to the side?"

"I'm somewhere in the middle."

*Of course!* I breathe heavily through my nose. "I will be there in a few minutes." I don't say goodbye and end the call.

I refuse to wander around anymore and back my car out of the parking spot. Leaning over the steering wheel so I can see the building letters, I make my way back around, trying to spot the section that 233 is in. However, I don't seem to notice, or remember, the speed bumps from my first time around. As I go over one, my chin slams into the steering wheel. I sit straight up and try not to cry as my lower lip quivers. I'm exhausted. I have to use the restroom, and I still have three more meetings today.

With tears welling in my eyes, I locate a parking spot, pull in, but keep the car running as the air-conditioning blows in my face. Although I have to use the restroom, I'm also nearing dehydration, so I take a long gulp of water and reach back into my cooler to remove a mini size chocolate-covered nougat candy bar.

Pulling my personal cell phone from my purse, I check that I've not missed any texts or calls from Aunt Paula. I remove the wrapper on a second mini candy bar and scarf that down just as fast as the first one. After another shot of water, I shove my bottle back into the cooler.

I shut off the car and glance through my windshield at the road on the other side of the complex. There is a man on a motorized scooter zipping down the sidewalk with an umbrella attached to the back and a Yorkshire terrier in his lap. My hand goes to my heart, and I'm reminded that no matter what, there is still joy in the world. And this man and his dog are enough to give me the energy to locate 233.

# Chapter 14

The rest of my day went by the same way it started, wandering into unknown places, being a sweaty mess, and managing bouts of hangriness. The one good thing about working in the valley was the places were closer together. It was nice not having to travel thirty miles from one meeting to the next. So outside of my clothes melting on me, it was a win.

I park my car at Palms Place, and as I'm walking in through the courtyard, the shimmering pool seems to shout *Jump in!* Clothes and all.

"Howdy, Kelly," a male voice says from behind me.

I jump and my keys slip from my hand. I pick them up and turn around to see George, per his name tag, dressed in Hawaii-themed swim trunks and flip-flops.

"Hey, does your place still smell like burned breakfast?"

"Thankfully, no." He leans forward as his eyes narrow. "Wowsers, you look beat. Want to join me in the pool? I can grab us some ice-cold beers."

I half-smile. "That sounds refreshing, but I should check in with my aunt and start dinner."

"Nonsense. I saw Herbert coming from Paula's place just a bit ago, and Carol said she stopped by, too."

I instantly feel unneeded, and slightly like a third wheel. And that's when I realize something. "Is everyone here single?"

George's brow furrows, and then his vision scans the courtyard. "Well, I'll be. Funny, I never noticed. But yep, nine apartments and nine singles. It didn't start that way. Vivian and her husband lived here; he passed away some years ago. And Fred, his wife, she died last year." His posture stoops. "So, what about that beer?"

"Thanks, but I really should get started on dinner."

"It looks like you don't have to." George nods across the pool at a resident coming in our direction.

"Rosa, number two!"

I can see George shake his head and lower his eyes.

Her hands are holding a colorful casserole dish, and the purse around her shoulder appears to cha-cha with each step closer. "You cannot see my name tag from so far." Rosa does a salsa move as her shoulders shimmy, and I smile widely. "I do the Zumba tonight. I've made you and Paula dinner."

She hoists the dish in front of me, but my hands are full of work papers, a laptop, and my cooler.

"I'll get that and carry it up for you." George takes it from Rosa.

"Thank you." I'm highly impatient, and surprises eat away at me like little leeches.

"They're late grandma's enchiladas." Rosa makes the sign of the cross over her body.

The warm aroma of the cheese and spices beneath the foil wafts out. All I can think about is holding a plate of enchiladas in one hand and a beer in the other while sitting on a pool floaty.

"Rosa," I whisper, "what happened to the dog you rescued?"

"I found a family through my bunco club. They wanted a small dog. Perfect match." Rosa beams and shimmies toward the main gate. "Tootles!"

I look at my full hands, then at the dish. "Thank you, but I can carry that up. Maybe just stack it on top?"

George gives me a frustrated look. "Why would I do that? I'm a gentleman."

I give a curtsy, and we walk toward the stairs. "Really, I would love to spend the evening relaxing, but I should organize a few things for work."

George pauses on the steps. "Do you work for free?"

I halt, almost running into him. "No, of course not."

"It's after five. Your work hours run past five?"

We continue up the steps and pass by Hebert's apartment, and I notice the blinds moving.

"No, I'm off at five, but it makes work easier for when I log on in the morning." I stop at Aunt Paula's front door and prepare the key.

"What about making it easier for you and your health? When do you have time to relax?" George clenches the casserole dish like he's not going to give it up easily.

"Relax?" I slide the key into the lock.

"You have every right to do as you please. But ask yourself, if you didn't show up tomorrow, or if you didn't organize anything tonight, will it make a difference? To the agency or to your manager? However, if you don't take time to relax, then it *will* matter to you and those who love you. Time isn't free."

George's words linger and attach to those said by Drew so many times in the past. *Work rules you, Kelly, when you should rule it.* I open the door, and I take a second to compose myself.

"Hi, Aunt Paula." My voice cracks.

She's sitting in her recliner, and *I Love Lucy* is on TV, again.

"George." Aunt Paula leans around the lampshade and smiles. "You cooked?"

He raises the dish and makes his way toward the kitchen. "I'd love to steal credit, but this is Rosa's doing."

"Please tell me it's her enchiladas?" Aunt Paula inquires as I shut the front door.

"Indeed." George comes back around the peninsula and looks at us. "I set them on the stove."

"George, why don't you stay and have supper with us," Aunt Paula says over the TV's noise.

I nod in agreement and set my stack of work on the kitchen table while tossing my purse on the chair.

"Only if you'll allow your niece to join me for a beer by the pool afterwards?" George widens his stance.

"I'd love to, but"—I glance over at my aunt—"*she* needs my help tonight."

"No. No, she's all yours, George." Aunt Paula reaches for the crutches resting against her recliner.

"No. *No.* Aunt Paula, that's silly." I say through clenched teeth. "I want to spend time with you."

"Hush, now. We'll eat supper, chat about the day, and then you can go." Aunt Paula stands up unsteadily but manages.

"I bet we can figure out a way to get you down those stairs, Paula," George offers.

"Figure all you want, but there is no safe way to get me down to the pool. I appreciate the offer, though." Aunt

Paula hobbles over to us. "Now, George, I insist, please stay."

He grins. "Alright, let me grab some beers back at my place."

"You read my mind." I head to the bathroom to splash water on my face, but when I look up at myself in the mirror, I'm saddened at what I see. I miss the pride I used to feel for myself. How I'd look in the mirror and be happy with who looked back at me.

Could I figure out a way to get back to the old me? The me I loved. Because that's what all those self-help books boast about. Love yourself so others can love you. The only question is, when do I find the time?

# CHAPTER 15

I feel bad about leaving Aunt Paula alone with Herbert, but as the water bobs around my waist when I enter the pool, I feel *less* bad. The wonderful thing about Palms Place is everyone is comfortable with who they are. My guess is when you've lived to be at least sixty, you stop caring what others think because you finally embrace doing what makes you happy. Hence, Vivian in a long button up shirt instead of a swimsuit. And why Fred has childlike orange floaties on his arms even though the pool at the deep end only goes up to his chin.

George dumped four bags of ice in it, causing the water to feel rather refreshing. The weather gauge attached to a pole nearest the pool reads 106 and it's eight o'clock at night. I glance up at Aunt Paula on the terrace when I faintly hear her laugh. To be fair, she is enjoying *a* pool. Herbert surprised her with a blue kiddie pool and Drumstick ice cream cones for everyone. George ran the garden hose up the stairs and filled it while Herbert carried two of the courtyard patio chairs with eighties green palm fan cushions up the stairs to sit on. Carol gave a disapproving eye when she spotted it, because tomorrow morning it will be blocking her walking path.

Of course, the page I took from the residents' book about being comfortable with my body vanishes like a cockroach when the lights come on as Aaron and Ransom stroll into the courtyard. I sink lower into the pool until my shoulders are under the water and hold my beer up in front of my face.

Aaron scans the environment as though he was there to give us all citations. George and I would get one for having alcohol in the pool, Vivian for dancing and playing the greatest hits album from the Steve Miller Band louder than it should be (although Herbert hasn't complained yet), and Beverly, has her caregiver within arm's reach, for her wheelchair being too close to the edge of the pool. I watch Aaron sigh. He looks beat, his shoulders pull forward as though trying to bury his neck in his shirt.

"Aaron! Come join us," George calls over "Take the Money and Run."

He looks directly at Beverly. "Should she be that close?"

"*Elle va bien*; the brakes are on, and just look at her smile." Vivian sways her hips.

And I'm jealous because I can't even move my hips like that without them sounding like a restaurant's pepper grinder.

Aaron and I lock eyes, then I avert mine, sort of like in school when I thought it might prevent the teacher from calling on me for the answer. Ransom leans forward, sniffing out the pool as though it holds his favorite toy.

"*Fuss*," Aaron commands.

Ransom snaps his head up, and together, with the dog heeling, they reach his mom's apartment door and disappear inside.

A part of me longs for Aaron's company, because I don't feel as though I have much in common with the rest of Palms Place residents. But the other part wonders if that's what happened with Drew. Wanting company, someone to talk to, but it turned into something more. Maybe it's why he didn't tell me the whole truth about what really transpired between him and the other woman, to keep from hurting me further. The damage was already done; the hurt was already there in my broken heart.

"I wish he wasn't so grumpy." George takes a long sip of beer.

"I doubt he's trying to be. If I feel completely exhausted after a day at work, I can't imagine how he feels." I lean my arm on the edge, setting my beer above the black-and-white four-feet tile marker.

"How is everything with your husband, with you being here?" George eyes the door that Aaron disappeared behind.

"Ah yes, I forgot y'all know thanks to my aunt." I run my wet hand over my hair, grabbing hold of the chunky strands at the base of my neck.

"She wasn't trying to invade your privacy, but I can see how it appears."

I raise an eyebrow in disbelief, but I also want to know if a group of widows, widowers, divorcées, and divorcés have any helpful advice.

"Drew, my . . . husband, and I have been struggling for some time. I want to work it out, but I don't know if we can fix what's broken or if we're postponing the inevitable."

"And why is it inevitable?'"

I stare at the water as it rolls up and down against my chest. "Because." I choke back on my words and try to continue. "Because after I found out what he did, it changed how I look at him. How I feel when he touches me, when he looks at me. Everything feels different, foreign, forced. As though I now question his love for me."

He nods his head but doesn't respond.

"I never thought I'd be one of those people who questions love, but I also didn't think I would ever have a husband who cheated. I thought, no, that's for reality television, and husbands who travel for work. And I know marriage takes dedication, understanding, and effort. But. . ." I stop myself before I mention the miscarriages I blame for causing the crack to form, because I'm on the edge of crying. "I *don't* want to give up."

My chin quivers and I lower myself further until it touches the top of the water. Maybe if I get my face wet, George won't notice it. "How do people stay married after something like this? How do you fix it and move past it?"

"I think you're looking at it the wrong way." George sets his beer bottle on the edge of the pool and his hands disappear under the water. "When I was married, my wife stayed home with the kids all day. We didn't have to compete with social media and cell phones. It was easier to find and make time. It wasn't easier, or harder, not to have affairs, but there was more time to be a family. Look around at all of us enjoying *time*. Do you see anyone on their phones around here?"

He's right. I've cut my screen time in half while being here. I don't even know where I left my cell phone. My purse? The coffee table?

"Today, everyone is go-go-go. They're all trying to get to their next destination or next project, the next big thing. Any free time we have, we fill it with chores, errands, or activities so we can post them on social media. How many times do you pick up your phone to check something during dinner or a movie?"

"All the time."

"All that time that could be spent *being* together."

"But cell phones and working hard didn't cause Drew to cheat. There was a fault in our marriage."

"And what influenced the fault?"

My chin quivers again. "Me."

"That's like blaming the volume knob for the radio being loud. Whoever turned it up is to blame. You're not the sole reason, no matter what you think. His choices were his to choose. Look, the changing world has made it more difficult to be who we should be, who we deserve to be for ourselves and those we love. Yet, sometimes, we're with the wrong person. And it's possible that we didn't know it was the wrong person until after the fact, when the world shows us. You can't make it work by forcing it. In the end, it must *be* right."

I bite the inside of my cheek.

"You give up things for your spouse, and he gives up things for you. Work takes over because we don't stay *mindful*. We stop loving ourselves because we become too busy trying to love each other. Yet, we make individual choices that we need to hold ourselves accountable for. And when you get back to loving yourself you can get back to loving others. When you truly listen to your inner voice, when you ask yourself the tough questions, you'll hear the answers."

George made sense, and I also don't like what he has to say. Who enjoys hearing the truth? It's raw and makes you feel exposed. The truth makes you vulnerable.

"Once you figure out the answer, you'll find the correct solution without regret or doubts." George interrupts my thoughts.

Tears well up, because I don't want to lose Drew. I want to find a way to make it work. But first, George is right, I need to stop blaming myself.

# Chapter 16

"If you don't get in that shower, I'm going to hose you down in the kiddie pool!" I glare at Aunt Paula as though I'm trying to shoot fire from my eyes.

"I don't appreciate your tone." She huffs.

"I'm sorry you don't like my tone."

"Let's talk about it." She mutes the TV.

"Oh, no, you're not getting off this easy any longer."

Aunt Paula raises her hand like the shrug emoji. "What? I just want to hear about your day, that's all."

"How about complaining? I'd like to complain about my day."

"Do that, then. You're very good at it."

I gasp at her insult, and flop onto the couch and lie down.

"Why don't you quit before you have a nervous break-down?"

"I can't quit. I have bills and half a mortgage. The entire reason Drew and I are living together during the separa-tion is because neither of us can afford to live on our own. I don't think anyone on one income can manage in this economy. Especially in Flag." I sit up. "And quitting is the same thing as failing, and I'm already failing my marriage."

"That's absurd logic. Who taught you quitting is the same as failing? Certainly not your mother."

I clench my fists. "Well, it feels the same. I want a job that makes a difference."

"You have a job that makes a difference."

"No, I don't."

"All I'm hearing from you is excuses. Excuses why you can't get a different job or apply for a better position. Excuses for Drew. Excuses for yourself."

I point my finger at her. "Wait a minute. How can you judge Drew? You did the same thing."

"I'm not judging him. I'm simply pointing out a fact. I never said Andrew should have forgiven me. I didn't make excuses for what I did, and he didn't make them for me. And I'm immeasurably blessed and grateful he chose to forgive me."

"And that's what I'm trying to do. Forgive Drew. Everyone makes mistakes."

"I'm not talking about forgiveness or mistakes. I'm talking about excuses. You've done nothing but blame yourself for Drew's infidelity. You're not the cause of it. Just as Andrew was not the cause of my affair."

"Okay, Aunt 'Refusing To Shower' Paula."

"I'm not refusing." She crosses her arms. "As I recollect, I said I'd do it later."

"You've been making excuses *and* refusing. I know you're afraid of falling again. That's why you won't shower."

"I'm not afraid."

"It's okay to be afraid."

The room is silent; outside, I hear voices. It sounds like Herbert is saying hi to someone. The air-conditioning kicks on, drowning out whatever else can be heard. Coolness filters through the room.

I stand up and kneel at the side of Aunt Paula's recliner, taking her left hand in mine. "You know, I applied for a promotional position."

"That's great. Why didn't you tell me?"

"Because if they call me for an interview, I'm not going to go, I changed my mind."

"That's ridiculous. It's only an interview."

"It's only a shower."

She takes long, slow breaths, in and out, as the clock tick, tick, ticks on the wall. "Kel, it doesn't feel that way to me."

"It's understandable. But I can guarantee if you don't shower soon, people will be afraid to be around you because you're going to smell like an old burrito on a hot day."

Aunt Paula tries not to laugh, but she can only hold her lips pressed together for so long. "Let's make a deal, then."

"Okay." I tilt my head.

"I'll shower if you go to the interview. You don't have to accept it if they offer it to you, you just need to do the interview."

"We don't even know if I'll get an interview."

"Kelly." She blinks forcefully to let me know I'm being absurd.

My heart races just thinking about it. I let go of my aunt's hand as mine grows clammy. There are things I hate about my job and things I love. But stepping outside my comfort zone when my life is a mess seems like the worst idea ever. She taps my hip with her good foot.

"Alright. I'll match your shower for a job interview, if it happens."

"It will."

"Please understand, Aunt Paula, I'll do my best to avert my eyes during the shower, while keeping you safe."

A warning beep comes from my cell phone, first my personal one and then my work cell. The thunder outside causes the living room window to rattle as I get up and check my phone to see two weather alerts for portions of Maricopa County: *Flash Flood Watch* and *Severe Thunderstorm Warning*.

I peek through the blinds. Flashes of lightning illuminate the courtyard from above.

"There weren't but a few fluffy clouds in the sky when I pulled in thirty minutes ago."

"Monsoon season. Is there a dust warning, too?" She leans forward in her recliner.

"Nope."

"Good. Oh, what's the temperature outside?"

I check the weather app on my phone. "Wow, it dropped quickly. It's only 100."

"Hurry, turn down the AC while we can. We can live it up at 78 until the storm is over."

I make my way to the thermostat when the doorbell rings, followed immediately by a frantic knock. "I don't have a good feeling about this." I'm at the door in a few quick steps and carefully open it as though a bolt of lightning will pop inside and set the carpet on fire.

"We need help to secure the furniture," Herbert raises his voice as thunder rumbles around him. "Aaron isn't answering his door."

I set both cell phones on the table. "Be right back," I tell Aunt Paula.

But I'm not right back. It takes a lot longer than I thought it would to secure lawn chairs, patio tables, and to cover the pool. And by the time I make it back to my aunt's apartment, I'm sopping wet and covered in leaves and pieces of palm tree bark. I run past her to the bathroom, hoping to keep as much water off the carpet as possible.

I emerge with a towel wrapped around my hair. "Alright, it's your shower time."

"Is it wrong to have hoped the storm would have blown you away?"

I grab her crutches, stand at her side, and hoist her up. "Yes. Yes, it is."

As we head towards the hall, Aunt Paula says, "You know I'm serious about you moving in. The spare room is all yours, once I finally unpack the last of my boxes. And as long as someone is at least fifty-five, you can live here."

I shake my head. "I appreciate it, but you have your own life. I can't intrude. I *won't* intrude."

"Maybe I need you to intrude."

"What are you saying?"

She leans forward on her crutches at the entryway to the bathroom as I flip on the light. "It wasn't only the costs and upkeep. I put the house up for sale because it reminded me of how lonely I was. How lost I felt in all the emptiness surrounding me. Carol said loneliness causes as many negative effects as smoking. Yet, even here, in this tiny apartment, with all these wonderful neighbors, I'm lonely." A tear rolls down her cheek. "I don't want to be alone anymore."

My aunt slumps, and I grab hold of her around the waist. The closest place is the toilet, so I guide her over to it and sit her on the lid. She's crying as I kneel on the bath mat in front of her.

"All your neighbors seem like friends that care about you."

"Yes, but I'm alone. Day in and day out. Meals alone, with some exceptions like FNF. And part of me wants to find someone and fall in love again, but I can't lose another husband. Look at me, I can't even care for myself. Having you here has been wonderful. Don't get me wrong, Palms Place is amazing, but I want to share my life with someone again. I need to share my life with someone."

I squeeze her hands in mine, but I can't say anything to make her feel better because it's all I want, too.

# CHAPTER 17

"Where is this darn house?" I make another U-turn and head back to where I came in at. The navigation shows the house should be right *here*, but it's a vacant, barren lot. I pull over, put my car in park, and open my laptop. The address I have matches what I put into the navigation.

I locate the client's number and hit the call button. It goes to voicemail, but they never bothered to set up a mailbox, so I can't leave a message. After disconnecting, it takes great strength to not toss my phone out the driver's side window. Maybe the house numbers are hidden or too small to see from the car. I grab my clipboard, laptop, and purse and step out, missing a puddle lining the curb from last night's storm.

I step over the stale water and onto the sidewalk. The sun's heat radiates off the concrete, and I wish I'd brought my water bottle. Every house appears to be crumbling in some way or another. Weeds grow high in yards and broken-down cars with flat tires or no tires at all sit in driveways. I observe each house, searching for a number, and spot cracked windows with masking tape over them or pieces of cardboard.

Then I hear it before I see it.

*Yap, yap, yap.*

The familiar bark belongs to a Chihuahua. I turn toward the noise and see four pounds of fiery fury charging at me. As though it's a bear and not a Chihuahua, I make myself bigger the best I can without dropping my laptop and clipboard.

I stomp my foot and shout, "No!"

We both freeze like a standoff at the O.K. Corral. Then I lunge forward without moving my feet to scare the dog enough to back off. A security door squeals open at the house to my left and a man in an open bathrobe, showcasing all his bits and pieces, appears.

"Lola! Lola, come here!" the man shouts at the dog.

The Chihuahua gives me one last snarl and then pivots and darts toward its owner. I expect a *sorry* or *oops* from the man whose dog almost took a chunk, small as it might have been, from my leg.

"You get in here right now, Lola." He steps to the side of the front door and the Chihuahua scurries inside.

I watch the door bang shut, and I let out a sigh. I might have avoided the dog bite, but I still can't find this darn house—*6420, 6422, 6426. Where is 6424?*

A car door slams across the street, and I glance over at the young man standing by the vehicle. "You lost, or are you planning to steal? You better not be trying to steal anything, lady."

I half laugh because it's ridiculous. "Yes, I don't like my Rogue anymore, and I'm looking to steal a better one."

He laughs. "Would be better if you stole my heart." He gives me a wink.

"I'll have to get back to you about that. Actually, I'm lost. Do you know where 6424 is?"

"It's that one right there." He points with his head at the house behind me.

I give him a wave. "Thanks." When I turn back around, there is no address to be found anywhere, not even on the side of the lopsided mailbox falling off its pole. Ants are milling around what appears to be a pile of vomit as I walk towards the front door. Creeping fig vines cover most of the front half of the dented garage door. Spider webs weave around the porch posts, and I don't know how I'm going to reach the door without walking through them. A phone book rests on the side of the worn welcome mat that reads WE OME. *When was the last time they gave out phone books?*

I use my clipboard to break up the spider webs and reach for the doorbell. There's noise coming from inside, so after a few seconds, I give the doorbell another push. But I don't hear the bell chime or anyone walking toward the door. I make a fist and rap my knuckles on the closest window, pounding like the police on TV dramas. Finally, the noise comes closer in the form of footsteps.

"Hold on!" a male voice calls from behind the door.

I step back from the window and check my shoulders for spiders. Instantly, the thought of them causes me to shiver as though they're all over me.

The door eases open with a horrendous squeal. "What do you want?"

I take a step back and move my clipboard to my side. "I'm Kelly from Sharon's Angels. Sorry to bother you, but I'm here to do the assessment."

"Yeah, I remember, but you aren't looking at me naked." He moves behind the door.

I wave my free hand in his direction. "No, sir, I just have some questions for you."

"Why?"

"Because you applied to see if you'd qualify for our services." It's dark behind him, and his eyes travel up and down my body, causing me to move the clipboard back to my chest.

"Fine." He leaves the door open and disappears down the hall.

I swallow and pinch my eyes closed, stepping forward. As I go through the door, something skitters to my right. I squeeze my clipboard closer to my chest and suck in a breath.

The sound of a classic Western show and flashes of light come from further down the hall. I locate the man, now in his recliner, the TV remote teetering on the armrest.

"Well, ask your questions." He doesn't look at me.

I spot a very full handheld urinal on this side table, along with a stack of mail and fast-food wrappers that have piled up. On top of the '90s wooden entertainment center are three framed photos of him with a woman. My cell rings and the ringtone tells me it's my personal phone.

While I remain standing, I ramble off my questions. Halfway through, I pause and glance at the photo next to him. "Is that your wedding picture?"

He doesn't look at it, his vision remains on the TV. "Married forty-three years to the love of my life, Kim."

"That's an accomplishment."

"We always said we wanted to go for fifty. How great that would be." His voice changes, his words are shaky.

"I'm sorry. You must miss her a lot."

He points at a frame on the entertainment center, one of the two of them on a white sandy beach with Windex-colored water. "She was my everything. I never realized how lonely I'd feel with her gone. How depressed." He looks around. "She'd be embarrassed having people over with the house looking like this. With me looking like . . . this." He runs his hand through what remains of his greasy hair. "You don't know how much I miss her hugs."

I'm sad for him, and it makes me think of my aunt. "I'm really sorry."

"Well, let's finish up."

I nod and ramble off the remaining questions I know by heart, scribbling down his answers as we go. Fifteen minutes later, we're done.

"Thanks for coming out here." He finally makes eye contact with me. "But sounds like I won't qualify."

"You're right. It appears that way."

"At least I had some company for a bit." He picks up his remote.

"Thank you for your time." I turn towards the door, but stop myself and swing back around. "Would you like a hug?"

His eyes slowly go to me. "Oh, no that's okay."

"Okay." I turn again.

"Can you at least help me with getting rid of the bed-bugs?"

I pause. "Bedbugs?"

"Yeah, I can't seem to get them to go away."

And that's when I allow my eyes to scan the room. Somehow, I'd missed the telltale sign—white powder lining the floorboards. My skin immediately itches every-where, due to my subconscious thoughts. *Crap.*

"Here." I flip through my clipboard and produce the community service flier. "There is a number you can call. They'll help."

"Thank you." He takes the paper from me. "Have a nice rest of your day."

"You too." I hurry to the door, yank it open, and nearly stumble outside. At home, I have a bin to put all my clothes in when I end up somewhere with bedbugs, but at Aunt Paula's apartment, I can't drop my clothes at her front door.

I unlock my Nissan and climb inside, punching the AC button to four. I run through my time in the widower's house. I didn't sit down, and he didn't have carpet. Did I come near the furniture? No, I stood in the middle of the room. Hopefully, that means I'll be okay. But I never know.

I remove my phone from my purse and see the missed call was from Drew, but he didn't leave a voicemail. I call him back, but he doesn't answer, and I don't leave a message either. I toss the phone on the passenger seat and pull out my work cell. It appears someone from the same number called me eight times in a row, a few seconds apart each time. I roll my eyes and check the clock on my dashboard. I must get to my next meeting, but it could be them calling to cancel, so I play the voicemail.

"This is Robin Comb. We have a meeting today for my mom, but the ambulance just took her to the hospital. I don't know what to do. Please call me."

I pull up her number from the missed call log. The line picks up on the first ring. "Hi, Robin, this is Kelly with Sharon's Angels. I got your voicemail."

"She's in the emergency room. Can you come to see her? I think they want to admit her and do surgery." Her voice is strained.

"I can see her at the hospital, but it sounds like we should wait until they get her stable and discharge her to a rehab center. How about I call you tomorrow, and we can go from there?"

There are hospital noises in the background, beeping, chatter, and overhead announcements.

"Umm, okay I guess, but you can't come out now? We're at Thunderbird."

Normally I know where every hospital and rehab center is in Flag, and while I assume she means Banner Thunderbird, as we often find some of our northern residents down there when our hospital can't meet the demand. Yet, I don't want to sound unprofessional. "I'm sorry you cut out. What hospital did you say?"

"Banner T-bird."

"Okay, well, hang tight. I can't get in the way of the nurses and doctors. Once she is stable, we can get her assessment done."

The line is silent.

"Robin? I'm really sorry. I wish there was more that I could do, but it's best to wait."

"Yeah, fine, thanks." The line goes dead.

I pull out my laptop and push the power button a little bit harder than needed. I feel so helpless as I add a note to my calendar to call Robin tomorrow.

After downing half my water bottle, I locate the nearest place to use a restroom. And it looks like it's going to be a home improvement store. But before I can pull out of the neighborhood, I notice something over the roofs of the houses on the street in front of me. I lean forward, gripping the steering wheel. A wall of dust is building, tan and puffy. My phone beeps an emergency alert and I grab it off the passenger seat.

*Dust Storm Warning* flashes with the caution triangle in the middle of my screen. Next, my work phone screeches with the same warning.

The car idles as my cell rings and Aunt Paula's photo appears on the screen.

"Hi, is everything okay?" My heart instantly races.

"Of course," Aunt Paula says. "I just saw an alert and I can tell you that the haboob just hit Palms Place and looks to be moving north. Where are you?"

"I'm not sure. I think I'm off Grand Avenue."

"Can you see the dust?"

"Yes." I watch as it continues to grow over the houses.

"It's rattling the windows here. I'm worried about you driving around in it."

"I'm parked outside of my last meeting. But I think the map shows my next one is going to be north of here, directly where the dust is coming from."

"The haboob will blanket everything soon enough. Can you call the people and let them know you'll be late? I don't want you driving in it."

"My next appointment was rescheduled, but I have a three o'clock one that's about twenty minutes from here."

"Alright, you can ride it out. And for tonight, why don't I see about cooking us something, that way you don't need to rush home?"

"Aunt Paula, you just started putting weight on your ankle. You're not standing at the stove, let alone using the stove. I'll bring home something. Hopefully, I'll see you around four, four-thirty." I glare at the house of bedbugs. "Although I'll need you to do me a favor. My car will be plenty hot all closed up, but I might have come in contact with some bedbugs today and don't want to wear my clothes inside your apartment."

"Don't you have another meeting?"

"Yes, but there is nothing I can do about that. Plus, it's at a rehab center and they always have threats of bedbugs, same with hospitals. They come in on patients all the time."

"I'm going to ignore I heard that."

"I want to make sure I don't wear my clothes inside your place or my shoes. Can you maybe leave me a robe or something that I can slip into when I get there? I can change outside if someone can hold open a towel to cover me."

"We'll figure out something. Do you have to deal with this often?"

"Yes, but I have a garage to streak through."

"I'm sure a few men around here won't mind."

"Aunt Paula!" My face flushes, and I think of the last time Drew joked about something like that with me. The last time he flirted with me. A lump forms in my chest so big it feels like a balloon. When I look down and notice the seat belt pressed around my forty-two-year-old stomach, I have to stop my thoughts from going there. It's not my fault. Drew should love me no matter what.

I look up and bite my lip. "I better get going; my eyeballs are floating."

"Love you, be safe."

"Love you, too. See you soon."

I set my cell on the passenger seat and turn my focus to out the windshield. The houses' roofs have now disappeared behind the wall of dust. Palm trees whip around, and birds fly haphazardly across the sky. A mesquite tree branch whizzes by, followed by an empty litter of soda, and a plastic bag flutters like a kite. The air grows thick like fog, and I know my bathroom break will have to wait. It's like a blizzard as far as visibility goes, and I can smell it coming in through the vents.

The dust storm swallows the Nissan. I can't see past the windshield. The wind blows and a sharp palo verde branch scrapes over my hood's paint. While I know I won't see a cow go flying by, I spot something and hear the dragging of metal. It's a lawn chair scraping down the street, and it narrowly misses the side mirror of my car.

I take another long drink of water and pick up my cell, deciding to give Drew another call. This time, he picks up on the fourth ring.

"Hey, sorry, Kelly, I'm about to go into a meeting."

"Yeah, I just saw I missed your call."

"Right. I wanted to talk to you about our mar—"

"Drew?" I pull the phone away from my ear to see the call has dropped.

A blast of wind causes my car to shimmy. My mind races with what Drew wanted to talk about. Was he about to say *marriage*? Not *separation* or *divorce*. Maybe if we went to counseling, I could work on forgiving him, and he could work on earning my trust back. I look at my cell's signal and see the dust storm must be messing with the strength of it, and the work hotspot never connects well with my phone.

I take a second to close my eyes and take a deep breath. Some days it seems I must remember to breathe. My stomach and chest hurt as though I've held it in all day, releasing it when I walk in the front door. And that might be part of the issue with my marriage falling apart. Finally breathing when I see Drew and laying my entire day in his lap, instead of reconnecting. Instead of focusing on being in love. I keep my eyes closed and remind myself to relax.

# CHAPTER 18

I pull into the Palms Place parking lot and keep my Rouge idling. It's raining outside, and I watch as the drops hit the windshield and run down like tears. The client I saw at the rehab center went on and on about the weather. He was a retired meteorologist who had way *too* much information to share. Not that I don't enjoy hearing stories, I just didn't have the time. I wondered if I'd seen him on a day that didn't involve a haboob, our meeting might've been shorter.

A knock on my car window startles me, and I turn to see Aaron standing in the rain. I roll down the window, not willing to get out yet.

"Why are you standing in the rain?" I tilt my head at him.

"Why are you not? It's a welcomed treat. So, bad day?"

"Where should I start? How about the meeting that should've taken twenty minutes lasted an hour and a half?"

"Sounds like a good meeting."

"Sure, if I was paid to lollygag." I wrap my hands around the steering wheel as rain drops splash inside.

"Well, are you working now?"

I check the time on my dashboard. "No, I'm done with my meetings for the day."

He sets his hands on the window frame.

"I need to make dinner for my aunt and I. Plus, I went into a house with bedbugs, so that's a whole thing."

"Just leave your clothes outside and take a shower."

I press my head into the headrest. "You probably come in contact with a lot of the same stuff I do."

He nods. "I've never had an issue, even with Ransom."

I peek around. "Where is he?"

"He's up with your aunt."

"What?"

Aaron laughs. And it's then I realize he's not in uniform. "It was my day off, and I noticed your vehicle was gone, so I figured I'd check on her."

For some reason—maybe the exhaustion of the day, or the hanger taking over, or the utter joys of perimenopause ruling my emotions—I start to tear up. "You checked on my aunt?" I can't look at him; it will only make it worse.

"Ransom insisted. Who am I to deny a K-9's wishes?"

"Oh, shoot!" I slap the top of my legs. "I forgot to pick up dinner."

Exhaustion continues to weave through me, deep in my veins, as though I just left an hour-long 1993 step-aerobics class.

"Don't worry about that." Aaron's hands are still on my window frame. "I can make something."

I turn, puzzled. Who is *this* Aaron? "Why would you do that?"

"Because you look like death."

My face flushes. "Gee, thanks."

He steps back, and I roll up the window. I pop open the door while grabbing my stuff. "You know, I work really hard, and this, this, Sun City—" I take a breath so I can continue with my rant. "It's hot, and not any hot, stupid hot. And when it's not raining, it's dusty. And somehow, it's still hot, even in the rain."

He crosses his arms, completely unfazed that I'm freaking out. "Do you always complain this much, or is it a Wednesday thing?"

"A Wednesday thing? I don't even know what that means." I'm breathing heavily, and the rain is dripping down my face, no doubt smearing my mascara. My laptop is wet, as are my clipboard and notes. My legs go weak, and I lean back against the Rogue, my bottom sticking to the wet door frame.

"You're getting everything wet." Aaron takes me by the elbow, as the rain drops grow bigger and heavier, guiding me through the gate and under the cover of the main arch into Palms Place.

"I'm aware." We pause, the mailboxes on either side of us. My socks are wet, and my toes feel like they're submerged in a bowl of chicken noodle soup. "My laptop is wet."

Aaron takes the laptop from me and looks it over. "Nah, it's good. You just got the top wet. The bottom was against the documents, protecting the vent. Maybe get a case for it next time?"

I take it back and shake my head. "I can't. Bugs. Bedbugs. I usually don't take my purse or laptop in with me, just my keys, phone, and papers. I leave the rest in the car."

"I won't remind you that's how things get stolen."

"Well, you know what types of places I go into, so you know why I have to leave everything in the car." I wipe my wet hair from my forehead.

"What are you in the mood for? Meat? Salad? Seafood?" Aaron looks at me as though he's really looking at me. Unlike Drew, who seems to look through me when we talk, because he can't bear to listen to me ramble on. I didn't realize it until this very moment. And Aaron is putting up with my emotions as though he doesn't want to throw his hands up and walk away.

"Kelly?"

"Yes," I shake the thoughts from my head. "Umm, food. Right. Dinner." I turn and look toward the pool as rain splashes down into it. "Something . . . comforting."

Aaron nods his head. "I know just what to make."

"No, really, you don't have to. I'll figure it out. You mentioned it's your day off. I don't want to ruin what's left of it."

"Don't assume." He looks around as though for something specific. "Hold on." He jogs out into the rain and opens his mom's apartment door.

I'm standing there, watching the rain under the cover of the mailbox area, taking in how it sounds different when it hits the pool water versus the palm tree fronds or the concrete or the roof's tile. Thunder cracks overhead, and I jump, sending my loose papers sliding down to the ground below.

I kneel on the wet concrete as the water runs like a stream into the mail area. I clutch the papers, wet and crumpled up. A shadow steps in front of me holding an umbrella. I'm reminded of that painting where the city lights and colors are muted from the rain and the person has their back turned to the artist, holding an umbrella.

Then Aaron does something that puts my heart in danger. He squats, resting the umbrella's stem on his shoulder. "I've been there. I overheard from apartment 3 who was talking to apartment 9."

"Ah, my separation is the talk of the complex." My chin drops to my chest.

"I wanted to save my marriage, but deep down inside, I knew it was already a loss. My wife had made her choice. It didn't matter what I said or did, because she was already gone."

My heart aches. I'm crying, and it's hard to hide. "I feel like I'm breaking into pieces. I'm not strong enough."

"Yes you are. You just have to find where you hid your strength." His hand reaches out for the top of mine that's resting on my left knee as my right clenches the papers. *How am I shivering when it's so hot out?*

"I don't blame her for the divorce," Aaron says. "When I came out of the fog, I realized it was the best decision for us. It took stepping away to see it. Doesn't make it easier or less painful. Doesn't stop us from arguing about the girls, but it takes away the self-blame, which is how you will heal."

"I never thought I'd be separated or . . ." I can't say it aloud.

"It's not like you're the only person in history to face a separation." He sighs.

"I have a lot of things I need to work out with Drew, and while I don't know if I can do it, I'm sure going to try."

"Then we better get dinner started, because sitting on the wet concrete won't cook the food."

For some reason, I find his comment hysterically funny. I laugh so hard I snort, and my body shakes, but not from the chill, from the relief that maybe something isn't wrong with me, that I'm normal, that I'm human.

# CHAPTER 19

I watch Aaron grab Carol from her apartment—not literally, but she holds his hand as they make their way up the stairs. In true Carol fashion, she's wearing a bright-blue sweater with a knitted cat's face on it and black yoga pants with puffy cream socks over the top.

"Here is your privacy screen," Aaron says and heads back downstairs while Carol holds up a large Hawaiian print beach towel. Because she's shorter than me, my head and shoulders are visible while I strip down and leave my rain-soaked clothes outside my aunt's apartment. Once inside, my aunt averters her eyes as I run naked past her and into the bathroom. I'm aware now more than ever that my body is not as lovely as it once was. Ransom's head pops up off the couch, his alligator stuffy next to him. From what I gather as I streak past, they've been sharing a bowl of popcorn. My stomach grumbles, reminding me I missed lunch.

I exit the bathroom as the aroma outside the door makes my mouth water. It's something I can't place, but the smell is inviting and comforting. I'm drying my hair with a towel as I enter the kitchen. Aaron stands at the counter, pouring two glasses of wine and something fizzy into a third wineglass. He glances over his shoulder at me.

"Wine for us, and I got an apple-berry-bubble thing for your aunt. My girls love these." He hands me a glass without fizzy bubbles.

I take it with both hands and want to hide away with it in the back room, along with a box of chocolate chip cookies. Instead, I sip and close my eyes. When I open them, Aaron is removing three bowls from the cupboard.

I return to the bathroom, hang the towel on the hook, and make my way back to the kitchen with my glass. "What did you make? It smells good."

"Pasta with roasted eggplant, goat cheese, and walnuts."

"Oh, that sounds . . . horrible." I make a face as though I've already had a bite.

He laughs. "No judgments until you at least try it."

I nod and peek at my aunt, pushing herself up. "Did you have a good day today?"

Aunt Paula is getting better with getting up from the recliner, without her crutches, and putting weight on her foot, but she still hasn't taken a shower. Her hair looks as greasy as the widower's from today's appointment. If I can't get her to agree tonight, I'm just going to shove her out the front door with a bar of soap and into the kiddie pool.

"PT was not fun, but it was wonderful to have Ransom's company."

I walk behind her to the kitchen table, when Ransom joins us, and follows behind. "I'm jealous."

My aunt lowers onto the dining room chair with a plop. Aaron sets the bowls in front of us. I raise an eye and fight the urge to push it away and just have wine for dinner.

"Trust me, it's good." Aaron pulls out a chair opposite me and sits. "When did you get clearance to put weight on your foot, Paula?"

"A few days ago, thank goodness. I was so sick of those stupid crutches, but I'm still getting used to my balance with this big clunker."

Ransom lays like the Great Sphinx between Aunt Paula and me. I pick around at the cavatappi noodles for a few seconds and then decide I'm too hungry and stab a bite onto my fork.

"Oh, gosh." I cover my mouth as I continue to chew. "It's . . . good."

Aaron smiles but doesn't say a word.

I grab his arm. "I mean, this is good."

He laughs and glances at my hand. "Thank you."

"Kel, is right, very impressive." Aunt Paula takes a sip from her wineglass. "How's it going with Herbert?"

"As soon as he sees Ransom and I, poof, he appears before I even slide my key into the lock."

"Still giving you grief?" I take a sip of wine, trying my best to slow down on the pasta as the void in my stomach feels as big as the depths of the Grand Canyon.

"Yes, and another resident that had a dog. I can't remember who, apartment 6 or 4. Frankly, I don't care who has a contraband dog. There are worse problems to deal with in this world."

"Rosa, apartment 2, and she doesn't have the Boston terrier anymore. She found a home for it." I lean back in my chair, allowing the merlot to warm me like a hug as I swallow.

A knock at the door causes us to turn our heads. Ransom is the first one up, followed by Aaron, and then me.

When Aaron pulls open the door, Herbert is standing there. "We have a problem."

# Chapter 20

"He couldn't have gotten too far. Has anyone tried calling him?" Aaron asks Herbert, who remains standing outside my aunt's front door.

"All we know is his door is wide open, and he's not inside. And he's not answering his phone because it's on his nightstand."

"What about his car?" Aunt Paula asks.

"It's in the parking lot." Herbert motions. "And the keys are on the hook in his apartment."

"Remind me which one Fred is again?" I ask.

"Apartment 5," Aunt Paula says, and adds, "remember the one showing signs of memory loss, possibly Alzheimer's."

Aunt Paula would know since Andrew had the diagnosis, and it took its toll on her, diagnosed at sixty-two and gone by sixty-four. Which seemed far too young, although it's more commonplace these days from the clients I've seen.

"Can you do a Silver Alert?" I ask Aaron.

"How old is he?" Aaron asks.

"Sixty-four," Herbert says.

"Does he have a diagnosis?" Aaron asks. "Or are you assuming it's Alzheimer's?"

"I don't know." Herbert crosses his arms.

"What about his kids? Would they know?" Aaron runs his hand through his hair.

"We've never seen pictures or heard him mention kids." Herbert scratches his head.

"Then a Silver Alert is off the table. The person must be sixty-five and have an official diagnosis. And only after exhausting all other resources looking for him first," Aaron mentions.

"That's dumb. How would you know what someone's diagnosed with? What about those who don't have family?" Aunt Paula snaps. "I need cookie dough." She pushes forward and grips the tabletop with both hands.

"No, I'll get it." I remove the tub from the refrigerator, scoop her some into a small bowl, and set it in the middle of the table. "After you finish your dinner, young lady." I spin toward the men and clap my hands. "Okay, let's make a plan."

"Great. *Fuss*." Aaron motions for Ransom to follow him. "Kelly and I'll round up everyone, check once more around the complex, then spread out into the community. We can use Ransom to trail. The rain will make the scent disperse, but he might get us going in the right direction. Herbert, let's get something that smells like Fred from his place."

"Even in all this rain, he can track?" Herbert points at Ransom.

"He's trained in trailing, using the ground or the air to locate the scent cone." Aaron grabs Ransom's leash. "Best grab a flashlight, Kelly."

Herbert rubs his hands together as though we formulated an evil plan. "I'll get everyone else."

I turn to my aunt. "Do you have a raincoat I can borrow and a flashlight?"

She points with her head toward the bedroom, and her expression is hopeless. I rest my hand on her shoulder. "Everything is going to be okay."

"I want to help."

"You are helping. He might end up back here, and we need someone to stay behind. Call me if you see him." I flip on the bedroom light and locate the jacket in the closet and see she has two similar ones. A cherry-red one and a canary-yellow one. Because I've never been a fan of red, I grab the yellow one.

"Do you want to finish dinner and relax in your recliner?"

"Relax? When a Silver Alert can't even be issued? No, I will not relax. I'll sit in the rain if that's what it takes."

"Flashlight?"

"Kitchen drawer by the dishwasher," her tone is robotic.

I grab the flashlight, check that it works, and thread my arm into the jacket's sleeve. "I'll be back, hopefully with Fred."

"Be careful."

I pause with my hand on the door. "I will."

The wind picks up, and the rain pelts me as I meet up with Aaron and Ransom by the pool. "Big Bird, how nice to have you join us."

I sarcastically fake laugh. "Funny."

Aaron elbows me and smirks. "Ransom is going to move fast, and probably do a lot of side-to-side swipes of areas. He's going to be all over the place, and we could be out for a while."

"I'm okay. I'm skilled at chasing around hospital staff."

He looks over my shoulder. I turn and see sparks of light on the ground as Carol makes her way over to us, along with Rosa and George.

"Carol, are your shoes flashing?" I point at her feet.

She glances down and makes a little jig to set them off. "Light-up shoes. Just another layer of protection for walking in the dark."

I smile. "Great idea."

"I'm going to take my golf cart and cover the ground to the south of us," George says.

"Good plan." Aaron points at George and Herbert. "You guys head down 135th"—then he points at Carol and Rosa—"you ladies head toward Meeker. Kelly and I'll take whatever direction Ransom wants to go, if we end up taking one of your routes, we'll switch so we can make sure someone is covering Greenview." Aaron presses his lips together as lightning flashes across the sky above us. "Every minute counts. Let's go."

I notice when I look up at my aunt's apartment that she's sitting on the terrace, in the red coat, just under the roof's overhang, but the rain seems to spray in every direction. *I should have left her with a bar of soap.*

# CHAPTER 21

The rain continues to pour from the clouds and the wind whips it around, making my aunt's jacket useless. Ransom's fur is sopping wet, but his nose continues to lead us forward as we follow what we all hope is the right direction.

"Still happy about standing in the rain now?" I ask as we move through what feels like rip currents of water around our feet.

"Maybe slightly less happy."

Then the K-9 stops. In front of us, the water is rushing down the street as though it's a small river.

"Dang." Aaron uses his hand to wipe the rainwater off his forehead. "Good try, Ransom."

"What do we do now?" I look left and right. "What does this mean?"

"His scent is muffled by the rain, there are too many scents coming off the wind. We should try to cross to see if he picks up something on the other side. But it's hard to say how long Fred's been missing and he could've gone in any direction."

I spot a church directly across the street in front of us, with houses to our left and a golf course to our right.

"Church?" Aaron asks.

I shake my head. "Maybe."

We stand there as the wind causes the palm trees to sway like they're made of rubber. The beautiful small church in front of us lets off a warm glow through the front stained-glass windows.

Ransom barks at the building, as we make our way across the rushing water.

"Do you think he might have gone in there?" He shouts over his shoulder as I catch up.

"Shouldn't it be locked?"

"It might be open."

"You're right. Maybe someone saw him wandering around and convinced him to come inside? A church I know of in Flag has Wednesday night service."

We follow Ransom as Aaron lets out more of the K-9's leash. There are no cars on the road, and unless the lightning flashes, the sky is smoke black. There was something about the church and its red double doors that gave me a little bit of hope. When we reach the front, I head up the three long steps. I look over at Ransom, soaking wet, nose to the concrete, who looks more like a homeless dog than a prized K-9 officer.

"I think God might forgive him for getting the church's carpet wet." Aaron gathers the leash a bit.

"I agree, he's an angel." I grab the door handle, but it doesn't budge. "It's locked."

Ransom lunges to our right and Aaron's arm yanks sideways, and we follow the dog who leads us down the long wheelchair ramp. Ransom sniffs back and forth, flicking across the pathway like Zorro's sword as we make our way to the side of the church. There are smaller buildings that have been added on with a walkway between them, and that's when Ransom lets out a loud whine and lays down near a man.

Aaron praises Ransom and removes a small ball on a rope from his pocket.

I approach the man, who is soaking wet. "Fred."

He has both his hands on the door handle and doesn't seem to notice us or Ransom. He's rattling the door so loud I can hear it over the rain.

"Do you know how to get inside?" Fred turns to us.

Aaron approaches Fred's side. "Why don't you come with us?"

"No, I'm late. I'm getting married today, but I can't get into the church. Do you know how to get in?"

"Fred, it's closed," I say calmly.

"Because of the storm? No, rain can't stop me from marrying Lissa." Fred yanks at the doors as the small half-inch gap between the frame and lock rattles in protest.

It's heart-wrenching to see him so confused that he thinks he's getting married, but I'm thankful we found him.

"Fred, why don't you come with us?" Aaron suggests firmly, as though he's going to arrest him.

This is not the way to approach Fred. It will only upset him.

Fred looks over his shoulder. "No, I can't, I'm getting married. I can't have Lissa thinking I don't want to marry her."

"She knows you want to marry her." I set my hand over his hand, and he stops jiggling the handle and looks at me.

"Do I know you?" Fred's eyes scan me. "Who are you?"

"I'm . . . I'm a friend."

"Of Lissa?"

I look at Aaron and then back at Fred. "Yes. Why don't we . . ."

We need to take him to the ER to get checked out. He's very confused, doesn't recognize me, Aaron, or Ransom. But Aaron is already holding his phone to his ear, and I fear that an ambulance showing up will make things worse for Fred. I shake my head vigorously at Aaron and mouth for him to hang up the phone.

"How about we sit down for a little bit?" I point to the wooden bench between the pathways that is somewhat protected from the storm.

Fred doesn't respond but allows me to take him by the arm and guide him to sit down. I pull out my phone and text my aunt to have her locate George and his golf cart so we can try to get Fred to the nearby ER. Even with the rain, it's at least 90 degrees outside, he might be dehydrated depending on how long he's been gone. Maybe he'll remember George and make it easier to convince him to get into something that doesn't have lights and sirens.

"Fred, can you tell me about Lissa?" I turn to him while Aaron stands by the door with Ransom who is still playing tug for his reward.

"Does he work here? Can he get us inside?" Fred looks Aaron up and down and tries to stand.

"Tell me about Lissa." I grab his hand and hold him down.

Fred's face lights up. "She's a real swell woman. She devours novels, smiles when she sees sunflowers, and she adores the rain." Fred looks out upon the empty parking lot as the drops continue to fall and the sky brightens after another lightning strike. "Do you think she's out walking in the rain and that's why she's late to the wedding?"

It kills me that I don't know anything about Lissa. Thankfully, we're saved by the bell, more or less. We're saved by a golf cart.

George comes flying into the parking lot, and I think he might have caught air as the tires hydroplaned toward us. The golf cart lines up with the sidewalk's lip and George hurries over.

"George!" Fred cheers and stands. "Have you seen Lissa?"

George shakes his head. "Sorry, buddy, I haven't. But come with me, and we can go look."

Fred stumbles forward, unbalanced. I grab him by the arm. Then George takes over and walks with him back to the golf cart, helping him into the passenger side. Before I can blink, George and Fred are heading out of the parking lot. Aaron, Ransom, and I remain under the cover of the pathway adjoining the two buildings.

"I hope it goes okay," I say. "He was pretty confused."

"Yeah." He crosses his arms over his chest. "I take it you deal with that a lot?"

"There really isn't anything I haven't seen. But the most common increase in sudden dementia-like symptoms can be caused by a UTI, even for men."

"And you don't have a medical degree?" Aaron smirks.

"I have a bachelor's in public health and psychology. When I started college, my plan was to become a nurse, but I decided I couldn't handle all the needles and gory stuff. Since I wanted to help people, I switched paths before I got too far along." I look at Ransom, who appears to be happy even though he's soaked.

"Let's head back." Aaron nods.

We try our best to not step in the small waves of water streaming all over the parking lot.

"Do you feel like you make a difference?" Aaron asks.

"No. Do you?"

"Not as much as I should."

"So, what got you into police work?"

"Love."

I choke on my saliva. "Love?"

"My ex-wife, before she was my ex, when life was all hearts and roses. I wanted to know that she was safe in our community, to keep the neighborhood safe by limiting and preventing crime. That way, if I was at work, at least I was trying to make a difference."

"That's really sweet. Of course, not the divorce." I place my hand on his arm for a second and then pull it back. "Do you mind if I ask why?"

"Her side of the story is that she couldn't handle my job or Ransom." Aaron looks down at his dog as we cross another newly formed river, unable to jump it. He holds out his hand and I take it so that I don't stumble, then he assists Ransom.

"And what's your side of the story?"

"She was tired of me," Aaron grumbles. "Eighteen years of marriage and that's it. She's just done with me. But like I said, once I stepped back, I could see it was for the best. No one should be forced to love someone."

It's then I realize we both married rather young. I think about Drew and me. Two miscarriages, jobs, and life, and how it all got in the way of love.

"You and your husband, you don't have kids?" Aaron asks.

"No."

"Is that by choice?"

"No, we wanted them."

"I'm sorry."

"Don't be. Life is given to us and it's up to us to make the most of it, no matter the situation. My job has really shown me what's important and how imperative it is not to waste time. I think that's why I'm struggling right now, because I keep wasting time, but don't know how to stop. Or I'm too afraid to stop. I'm not sure which one it is yet."

"I hear you. My girls, gosh, I miss them so much, but they'd rather live with their mom. I can't even get a decent house for them to come and stay with me on the weekends. The house prices are manageable right now, but my child support payments are high. I'm not complaining, but it's hard to get by on a single income."

"You don't need to tell me. I have a social worker's income."

Aaron laughs. "I see so many exes still living with each other because they can't afford to live on their own, or they tried to move out and ended up moving back. There has been an increase in domestic calls over the years."

"That's sad."

We continue our rain-soaked walk back to Palms Place. And just as we approach the apartment's parking lot, a loud snap comes from above. Something long and large is falling fast. There's a crunch and the sound of shattering glass.

Aaron, Ransom, and I jump back.

"Oh, no!" I wave my hands at the destruction in front of us. "No, no, no, no!"

A palm tree has fallen and now looks like a hot dog in a bun. The problem is the bun is my car.

# CHAPTER 22

I have no clue how my aunt drives *this* vehicle. It's like a tiny engagement ring box teetering on four Super Swampers. I turn her Jeep into the neighborhood where my final meeting of the day is located. I'm behind on typing up my cases, and I still need to get ahold of Robin Comb to reschedule her mom from the other day when she went into the hospital unexpectedly. I do like that I can see better sitting up high in the Jeep, but it also makes me feel wobbly and off balance. My Rouge, or what is left of it, is still sitting under the fallen palm tree as the insurance company works on the claim. Of course, the *best* time to find out you don't have rental car coverage is *after* you need it. But Aunt Paula was nice enough to trust me with her Jeep. Not that she could climb into it right now. Trying to get into it this morning had me looking like I was mounting a horse.

"Wow," I mumble as I turn down another street.

The houses are all one-story ranch styles, but it's not the typical track-home-filled street. Instead, each one is a custom design. One beautiful house stands out, all white flat stucco, but it's surrounded by historic houses, so it looks utterly out of place. When I pause to think about all the awesome houses I'm allowed to go inside of, it makes me love my job, for a few seconds. And it's fun to drive down the road past towering mansions and historic houses knowing what the inside of them looks like. Especially one that housed a late Hollywood celebrity's daughter. But it's also allowed me to realize that everyone needs help at some point in their life. Just because a famous parent dies doesn't mean they leave the money for their offspring. The downside is driving past shacks and apartment complexes that should be condemned and knowing what the inside of those look like, too.

I ease off the Jeep's gas pedal as I turn onto the next street. The navigation on my phone tells me the house is located three down. And I can't help but do a jig in my seat as I spot the house. It appears to be inspired by Frank Lloyd Wright. Thin strips of windows and a covered straight side porch leading up to a retro French door with detailed carvings that can be seen from the street. I gather my laptop and clipboard, knowing I shouldn't have any issues with bedbugs.

I straighten my T-shirt and hope I'm not sweating so much that it's noticeable. This house is nice, and I don't want to stick to their furniture. I also try to wipe the envy from my face. This is the type of place I always dreamed I'd live in, a place to call home and build a family in. My house in Flag is livable, but it needs major repairs, and Drew and I haven't been able to afford them yet.

I push the doorbell and hear it chime through the vastness of the house behind the doors. Taking a deep breath, I look around at the patio's potted plants in bold blue containers and a water feature trickling under the doorbell. When I called to set up the meeting, we talked for less than a minute to confirm the address, time, and date. I find, in most cases, the nicer the house, the more resources they have at their disposable, which means they're either very rude because they expect to get services or super nice because they don't need them.

A woman dressed in shorts and a cute flower T-shirt eases the door open. "Hi, you must be Kelly, I'm Carrie. Come in, come in. It's far too hot out there." She waves me into the foyer, and I'm surprised and delighted that she calls me by my name without having to introduce myself. Usually no one remembers my name. Half the time, they don't even remember our appointment.

"Thank you so much, Carrie. It's nice to meet you." I step onto the worn but shiny terra-cotta tile that spreads from the front door into the formal living room.

"My mom is in the family room." Carrie's bare feet pad down the hall into the next room. "Mom, Kelly's here."

I follow behind as the hall opens into the kitchen and family room combo. Fake candles flicker on the fireplace mantel, and classical music with ocean scenes plays on the TV.

"We need to see all the water we can during the summer." Carrie approaches an older lady sitting on the plush tan leather sectional. "You must be thirsty. Let me get you some water. Unless you'd like some iced tea? We have regular, peach, and raspberry."

I shake my head. "Oh, water will be just fine. Thank you." I look at her mom. "Hi, I'm Kelly."

"Oh gosh, my manners. Kelly, this is my mom, Debbie. Mom, this is Kelly. She's here to see if we can get you some services." Carrie walks back toward me with the water, and I take the ice-cold bottle. "Sorry, I'm so used to opening them for my mom that I twisted that one's cap already."

"Thank you, no worries. Where shall I sit?" I ask.

"Anywhere you want. Do you need the table, or . . .?"

"I can sit here." I point to the couch. "That way your mom is close."

"Perfect." Carrie folds her left leg under her as she sits down next to Debbie. "Gosh, are you hungry? Can I get you something to eat?" She leans forward like she's going to stand up.

"I'm okay, thank you so much."

"Are you out in the heat a lot?" Debbie's voice is soft yet raspy.

I nod my head and take a sip of water. "Not normally. I live and work in Flagstaff. I'm only down here for a little while to help my aunt."

"I'm sure she feels blessed to have you," Debbie adds.

"I sure hope so." I laugh, and they both smile.

Then I dive into my questions, scribbling down their responses as my hand cramps. Being around such a loving mother-daughter relationship is hard from time to time. I miss my mom. I swallow my emotions before they surface and close with Debbie's medications and the list of her doctors.

"Thank you for allowing me into your home. I'll reach out in the next few days with the determination." I stand from the couch and observe their expressions. Are they upset, indifferent? At least I won't have to back out of the home like I did when that one client got out his gun.

"Thank you for your time, Kelly. Can we get you anything to take? Another water?" Carrie points at my almost-empty water bottle.

"I'm okay, thank you, though. It was nice to meet you both."

I follow Carrie to the front door, but she doesn't open it. She sets her hand on my arm. "My mom won't be eligible for services, will she?"

Of course, I already know she won't but breaking the news to people when they're standing directly in front of you usually doesn't go well. I prepare myself. "I don't think so." *Here it comes!*

"It's okay, Kelly. We appreciate your time. In fact, it's a good thing. It means she's doing better than I thought."

Clients and families rarely say these words. I release a held breath. "Thank you for being nice about this."

Carrie shakes her head. "I can imagine how these normally go." She opens the door. "You don't get the appreciation you deserve. But my mom and I thank you for your time."

I step out into the heat and sunshine. "Thank you. Remember, if anything changes, we can always reassess her. Have a nice rest of your afternoon."

"You too." Carrie closes the door so quietly I don't hear anything until the lock slides into place.

I take a deep breath and feel light in my steps. Having a meeting with kind people always makes such a difference in shaping my day. I climb into the Jeep and pull out my notepad. I need to give Robin a call and see if I can swing by Banner Thunderbird and get her mom's evaluation completed. On the third ring, she picks up.

"Hi, this is Kelly with Sharon's Angels. Is this Robin?"

"It's me."

"Hi, Robin. Is your mom still at Banner? I'd like to swing by if possible."

"She died last night."

Suddenly, my peacefulness melts like an ice cube on the Sun City sidewalk. I've been in Robin's shoes and they're right back on my feet as if I were nine all over again.

# Chapter 23

As I climb down from my aunt's Jeep, I spot a dog in the corner near the entrance gate of Palms Place. The pavement must be over 150 degrees. I leave the driver's side door open so that shutting it doesn't startle the dog. It freezes when it hears me, and that's when I notice it's not a dog. It's a coyote.

"Crap," I whisper, and reach back for the door. "Never mind." I scramble up into the Jeep's driver's seat and slam the door closed.

George's golf cart pulls in next to me, and he's wearing yet another Hawaiian shirt. I roll down the window to warn him of the coyote, just in case he didn't see it.

"Everything okay?" He leans across the seat.

"Coyote." I point. "I thought it was a dog."

He follows my finger, and then he turns back to me. "No problem." He grabs something off the dash, and it's followed by a loud siren blast.

The coyote runs off, and George waves me out of my hiding spot. I ease out from the Jeep, afraid the coyote is going to return with a group of friends.

"That's why I always carry one of these." He holds up a canister that looks like spray cheese in a can with a mini red horn on the top. "That's another reason we try to keep the gate closed. We all want a swimming buddy but must draw the line someplace." He chuckles.

"Hey, you never know, he might have been a good listener." I grab my stack of papers, laptop, and purse, then lock up the Jeep. George is waiting when I turn around, and I crane my neck to make eye contact.

"How was work?" he asks as we walk together toward the gate.

"Sad. A client I was supposed to evaluate passed away." I step up onto the sidewalk. "Oh, how is Fred doing? Did they end up admitting him? I haven't seen him around."

George opens the gate and closes it behind us. "They're keeping him a few days. I guess he's dehydrated, and they're running some tests because of his confusion."

"He's fortunate to have all of you." We walk past the mailboxes and toward the courtyard and spot Carol doing laps in the pool.

"We're lucky to have each other." George stops in front of the pool as Carol stands up in the shallow end. "Except for Carol, of course."

"Except for Carol what?" she asks.

"We were saying how great it is that we have each other, but, Carol, you're such a pain. We don't care for you too much." George smirks, and Carol narrows her eyes.

Then her hand comes up and I jump to the side as the chlorinated water lands on his flip-flops, splashing George's legs. He chuckles, removing his Hawaiian shirt.

"You're going to get it now." He tosses his shirt on a nearby chair and hurries down the stairs into the pool. Carol laughs as she swims away.

Their laughter follows me up the stairs to my aunt's front door. I unlock it and enter to find her asleep in the recliner, but I wake her up when I shut the door behind me.

"Hi, Kel, how was work?" She sits up and rubs her right eye.

"We still have wine, right?" I laugh.

She doesn't laugh. "Can we talk?"

I place my workload and purse on the kitchen table. "Is everything okay?"

"Are you still on the clock?" she asks.

I check the time. I'm off for the day, but I have a ton of typing and medical records to request. I'm falling behind, yet again. It's going to be a late night.

"I have all the time in the world for you." I kneel at the front of her recliner and grab her hands in mine. "What's going on?"

She starts to cry. "I'm scared."

"About what?" I let go of her hands and give her an awkward chair hug.

"About being alone, like Fred. What if that happens to me, and I'm not found?" She punches her fist into the top of her thigh.

Tears stream down my cheeks, and I don't realize I'm crying until they fall on the top of her shorts, soaking in like wet paint on a thin canvas.

"Why are you crying?" she asks through her sobs.

"Because I'm afraid, too."

My aunt leans back in the recliner. "Afraid of what?"

"What my future with Drew will be. What I'll do about my job." I crumple back into a seated position on my knees.

"What can I do to help?" She squeezes my hand.

"I wish I knew. I'm . . . burnt out. But I'm too scared to do any other job. I'm scared about not being able to fix my marriage. I'm just scared. After all these years, I still don't think I know how to be an adult. I'm tired of crying and scared that I won't get the chance to be a mom."

Aunt Paula eases back into her recliner, and she shuts her eyes. The wall clock tick, tick, ticks as loud as the heartbeat in my chest that vibrates up to my eardrums.

"I wish I could understand how you feel about not being a mom. It was never a desire of mine to have children. And I wish I could offer you a glimpse at your future, Kel. To let you know that it's going to be alright, no matter what. The thing about life, from what I've learned is, you don't know the answer until you take the leap. And sometimes you don't know until you fall and get back up. You've always been very good with excuses. Is there a job where you could use your excuse-making skills?"

"Hostage negotiations?" I grin. "Now, don't take this the wrong way, because I know how it comes off. I'm not *old* old, but I'm not young anymore."

She crosses her arms.

"Forty-two is midway." I close my eyes and take a deep breath. "Forty-two seemed so old when I was in my twenties. Now it seems young for some things but too old for dreams."

"Why do you believe that?"

"Too many risks, too many complications, and with my history—I don't want to use it as a bandage for my marriage."

"And does Drew have anything to say about this?"

"He shrugs his shoulders and says we can discuss it later, but . . ."

"Later never comes."

I nod.

"Leave Drew out of the picture. What do you want? And not the answer you think you should give. The truth you'd write in your diary because it's the only place you could be honest without judgment."

"I want to feel loved. I want to feel beautiful in the way I did when I was younger. I want to feel good about the work I do, and I want downtime, where I can relax and have time to live life. I want a family."

"And can you do that with Drew?"

I pinch my eye closed and see his face, but also see *her*. "I know I don't want to give up."

I hear a giant splash in the pool as though someone has done a cannonball, and Carol screams with laughter.

"Well, I support whatever you decide is best for you." Aunt Paula turns back to me.

"How about some edible cookie dough?" I stand up.

"Sounds great."

"On one condition."

"I know, the shower."

"I promise I will *not* let you fall."

I guide her to stand. She's always stiffer if she's been sitting for a while. "Doesn't make it any less scary."

"I know."

# Chapter 24

"She showered!" I tell Aaron as he stands in front of the dumpster. "Sorry, I'm so proud of her. I had to tell someone." I stoop and pet Ransom, gazing into his amber eyes that always seem to see deep into my soul. "Ransom, has anyone ever told you how handsome you are? Handsome Ransom." I can't help myself and give him a kiss on his forehead.

The sun is already well over the horizon as I move toward Aunt Paula's Jeep. I only have one meeting today, and probably four to five hours of typing when I get back. No matter how much I do on my own time I can't seem to catch up.

"That's great, about the shower. I wish everyone I ran into on patrol was that eager about being clean." Aaron loads Ransom into the back of the already running cruiser.

"I always wondered how you they keep dogs cool in there."

"There's a system that monitors the interior in the rear and front of the vehicle. It automatically averages the temperatures and triggers the air-conditioning when it goes over 75 degrees. There is also an engine-stall feature."

"That's high tech."

"I wouldn't have it any other way. It's not just me I have to look out for and monitor heat-related issues. I can climb out of the cruiser and not worry about my feet touching the pavement, but I must worry about his paws. I'm glad he doesn't throw a fit when he wears his rubber shoes."

"You really love him. He's lucky. I've seen too many not-so-great things with clients' dogs out there. I report them, even if it risks an issue getting back to me."

Aaron looks at Ransom, whose head is sticking out of the back window, his drool rolling down the outside of the glass. "I guarantee he loves me more. We would do anything for each other." He grins and gives Ransom a rub on the head. "I love him more than I ever loved my wife."

I gasp and cover my mouth. "That's . . . well, I can understand that."

"You know how some people say home isn't a place, it's a person?"

I nod.

"I think home is wherever your dog is."

"What if someone doesn't have a dog?"

"Then they should probably get one."

I laugh and feel sweat forming in the middle of my back. "Do you have days when you already assume your shift is going to be out of control?"

"Yes, full moons are the worst."

"I've heard that from some nurses in the hospital. That and Friday and Saturday nights in the ED are the worst."

"ED?" Aaron asks.

"Emergency department. Depending on the hospital. Some places it's ED, some it's ER. It drives my boss nuts when I switch back and forth in my reports."

He blushes. "I feel like I'm in college when you're around."

"That's a good thing?"

"I think so." Aaron nods and lets out a sigh. "So, how much longer are you staying in town?"

"I'm not sure, my aunt is getting better. I really should head back home to Flag, but my boss says Maricopa County really needs the help. There are just not enough workers to cover all the applications coming in."

"Speaking of work."

"Right, well, have a safe day." I open the Jeep's passenger side door and drop my purse and laptop on the seat.

"You too. I don't want to have to come rescue you."

I climb inside and shut the door, pondering why his words mean more to me than they should. *Rescue me.* I suddenly want something to go very wrong so Aaron can rescue me. Because I know Drew never would. In fact, I've needed Drew before, but he must not have been in the rescuing mood. Or maybe I wasn't worth rescuing.

I don't have to be familiar with a town to know what parts of the cities are dangerous. Shoes hanging overhead on power lines. Dogs running loose. Trash cans knocked over with junk spread around and no one bothering to pick it up. The ghost town feeling on a populated street. These are all dead giveaways.

The navigation tells me I'm here. Yet, I'm not sure where exactly *here* is. Sure, there's a house I can see out the Jeep's passenger window, but that place should be torn down. I climb from the Jeep and look around. It's dead silent. The leaves on the ironwood and acacia trees aren't even rustling. I step onto the sidewalk as a pit bull comes charging from behind a chain-link fence. He's snarling and lunging at me through the links.

"Hi, buddy, I hope you have enough water and shade." I give him a little wave. I never blame the dog for being a dog. He's protecting what's his, and I'm a stranger.

Concrete radiates the heat back at me as I approach the low gate at the house one down from the pit bull. There's no address number on the curb or the house. But the picture of the house on the navigation matches.

I place my hand on the gate and check the yard for animals. I learned many years ago that dogs are not the only thing that can come around the corner of a house.

The front door beyond the overgrown bright-pink bougainvillea opens, and a woman about my age steps onto the patio. "Hey, there."

"Hi, I'm Kelly from Sharon's Angels."

"Good, we've been waiting." She holds out her hand as I approach the two steps up to the front porch.

"Sorry, I wasn't sure . . ." I look behind me. "I didn't see an address." I shake her hand.

"Neighborhood kids, we put those reflective stickers on the beam here, but they think it's fun to remove them, so the pizza delivery driver gets lost." She steps inside and I follow. "My dad's out back."

The house's walls are made of plaster, and they've cracked everywhere. The place has never been remodeled, and it shows. Every décor style appears original to the sixties as we head through the kitchen and out the slider into the all dirt backyard.

Off the covered patio, to my right, is a tiny blue kiddie pool like the one Herbert got my aunt. This one holds a white plastic chair, and a hose is draped over it. I suspect this must be where they shower their dad. The first time I was introduced to this type of care, it shocked me, showering a loved one in the backyard pool. But often it's necessary because either the shower inside the house doesn't work or the shower chair is too big to fit in the shower.

The woman approaches a shed, gives a solid-fisted knock, and then opens the door. I follow her inside. It's unbearably hot, worse than standing outside. The fan on the dresser is not helping, other than to keep the flies from landing on it. Directly in front of me is a twin bed, where the man in his eighties sits on the edge. The man looks comfortable, as though he's not bothered by his living arrangement. He's dressed in jeans, suspenders, and a food-stained white T-shirt. A mini refrigerator works as a dual-purpose nightstand. There is a dresser to my left and a toilet in a closet size opening next to it. The woman stands in front of the counter that contains a hot plate and a single-basin sink.

"Dad, this is the lady I told you about. She's here to do your evaluation." The woman raises her voice, and I glance at the man as he leans forward. He gives a nod, then looks back at me.

I ramble through my questions, raising my voice to where I know I'll need Tylenol and hot lemon water when I get back to my aunt's place. Flies keep landing on the man's face and arms, but he doesn't swat at them. I'm right about the pool. It's for his bathing. Per our conversation, he refuses to live in his daughter's house because he doesn't want to burden her.

The daughter rolls her eyes. "I've told you, Dad, you're not a bother."

"I take it you're looking for placement, then." I lower my voice just in case this upsets him. Over the years, I've had some families agitated with me about letting the cat out of the bag that they want their parent out of the house.

She nods and crosses her arms. "I offer to help him, but he refuses. I can only try for so long. I have a husband and kids, so I don't have time to fight with him. He's always been stubborn."

I finish gathering the information I need from them and then hand the man my pen to sign two pages of documents. As he's signing, I notice the dirt and grime under his nails. Plus, he coughs and uses the pen to cover his mouth. He hands the pen back up at me with the papers.

I take the papers. "You keep the pen. It's a souvenir." I smile.

He seems pleased, as though he has a million things he needs to write down.

The daughter walks me back to the front door, and I thank her for their time, but she doesn't offer me water, even though I'm sweating horribly.

I give another wave to the barking pit bull at the fence and climb into the Jeep. When I remember I don't have any more meetings today, I climb back out, take a water bottle, and dump it straight over my head. The cold water shocks me, giving me the energy I need to spend the rest of my day in front of my laptop. The great thing about the lack of humidity is nothing gets moldy, so any water that ends up on my aunt's seat will be dry before I even pull into the parking lot.

As I gather my work items, I spot a familiar white Dodge truck in the Palms Place parking lot. I shake my head at the thought and halt just past the mailboxes. Why would *he* be here? It's about a two-hour drive without traffic and the I-17 is always jam-packed this time of year.

It's a mirage. It must be a human-shaped mirage.

"Kelly, hey."

"Drew?"

"My word, it's hot." He looks like he stepped out of JC Penney's catalog from my childhood.

For a second, I think he said I'm hot and I smile, but it fades quick as I realize he meant the weather and not his wife.

"What are you doing here?" I slide my aunt's key into mailbox number seven.

He pulls his head back, making his neck and chin almost become one. "I came to— Can we go somewhere and talk?"

"Why didn't you return my calls or text from the last few days?"

He stands uncomfortably in front of me and doesn't answer. "Can we talk?"

"Sure, um, do you want to grab a bite to eat?" I point outside of the Palms Place gates.

"I'm not hungry." Drew shakes his head.

I felt like we should've hugged when we first saw each other. Separation or not, we hadn't seen each other in over two weeks, but he didn't appear to *want* to be close to me. He keeps his distance. I envision myself as that elderly man with flies on my face. Alone.

"Okay." I motion to the courtyard.

We make our way to the patio furniture, and we pull out chairs. The legs scrape on the concrete, no doubt alerting every Palms Place resident.

Drew sits and I do the same, setting my work items on the tabletop. "I talked to a lawyer."

"About the separation? I didn't think that was necessary. It's not like I'm going to take all your stuff. We still live together." Sweat is forming under my arms and down my back. My legs feel like they're gluing themselves to my pants.

"No." Drew looks at the table and plays with his keys, the noise echoing around us. "I realized, while you've been gone, that I don't miss you like I should."

I open my mouth to say *oh*, but nothing comes out, because I've lost my breath altogether.

"I guess this time apart helped me see something was missing between us. I'm not saying I didn't make a mistake, and that I don't feel bad, but I've realized what we have isn't . . . isn't working. I'm sorry it happened this way."

Tears form in my eyes and I'm trying not to allow my body to shake, but it seems impossible.

"Kelly, the lawyer is for a divorce." He leans forward. "I do feel bad about all this."

"You feel . . . *bad?*" I whisper over the sharp pain in my throat, and dizziness washes over me.

His jaw clenches. "I didn't see how unhappy I was. I think you should have seen it, too. Kelly, we haven't been working for some time now. Maybe if we had been able to have kids, it would've been different."

"We?"

"We don't have to suffer anymore. We can live our own lives and be happy."

"Happy?"

"It might take a bit, but you'll see this is for the best."

I shake my head. "You don't want to try to fix us?"

"There's nothing to fix. Kelly, you know I'm right. Don't you want to be happy? And I don't mean 'getting by' happy."

I can't answer him. I wipe tears off my red-hot cheeks even though I feel lightheaded. *Low blood pressure. Take a deep breath.*

"People change, people grow, and some things don't continue working the way they once did. We don't need to waste any more time. I found a friend to stay with. We can put the house up for sale, and while I doubt there will be a profit, we can at least get out from under it."

Drew places his hand on my shaking left knee. "Kelly?"

Everything around me spins. The pool seems to float in front of my face. "Oh crap, not again." Then, I black out.

# CHAPTER 25

"Ms. Kelly? Ms. Kelly?"

I feel a hand on my shoulder.

"Ms. Kelly?"

I ease my eyes open, woozy.

"Ms. Kelly? Herbert here."

I try to sit up and realize I'm already sitting. When my vision comes into focus, Drew is across from me. But I'm no longer in a chair. I'm on a lounger near the pool.

"You slid from your chair when you passed out," Herbert says. "Don't worry, no calcium canyons were involved."

I put my hand to my shirt and realize it's soaking wet.

"We splashed pool water on you." Carol leans over me. "Your pulse was very shallow."

"We need to get her inside, in the air-conditioning." I recognize Drew's voice and scowl.

"I think you're right. *We* do. Not you," Carol snaps.

I try to lean forward and notice that all of Palms Place, minus Aunt Paula, is hovering around the lounge chair I'm occupying. When I spot Drew, the wooziness returns.

"Divorce," I growl, then whine, "Carol?"

She places one hand on my shoulder and the other on top of my arm. "Yes, dear, we'll make Drew leave."

I shake my head in slow motion. "He wants a divorce," I spit. "He made a mistake, a sixteen-year mistake."

"That's a pretty long time for a mistake." Carol rubs my arm. "You should really stop passing out."

"I have low blood pressure issues." My shock and sadness turns into anger, a mighty river finally breaking free from its path to crash headfirst into the rapids.

"You're the one who cheated." I groan like the Demogorgon from *Stranger Things*. "I should be divorcing you!"

"Is there a problem?" I see Ransom before I spot Aaron.

"No, no, no," I whisper and swing my legs over the edge of the lounge chair, but Herbert holds my shoulder, preventing me from standing as I sway.

"There is. Please get this man to leave." Carol crosses her arms. "He's not welcome at Palms Place."

Rosa moves the cigarette from between her lips and leans toward Aaron. "That's Kelly's soon-to-be you-know-what."

"And we'll help you," George says. His height causes him to tower over Drew.

Herbert steps forward toward Drew. "We asked you to leave, Mr. Drew."

Drew raises an eyebrow, surprised by the hostility from a group of elderly people.

"*Bellen*," Aaron says toward Ransom. This causes the English Labrador to bark at an ear-piercing level that causes me to cover my ears.

Drew puts his hands up and backs away, heading toward the mailboxes without turning his back to Ransom until he's beyond the gate.

"Now, let's get you inside." Carol takes me under the arm and helps guide me to standing. "We can figure all this drama out later. Men, am I right?"

As Carol is on one side of me and Rosa on the other, we make our way around the pool, and Aaron gives me a look of confusion. I mouth, "Tell ya later." He nods in response. And a part of me, for a second, wonders if Drew is right in his decision.

I cry before I step into the shower. I cry during the shower. I cry when I get out of the shower. And I'm still crying when I head into the living room to find Carol, Vivian, and Rosa have been keeping my aunt company.

"Kelly," they sigh in unison as though I lost an arm in the shower, and it washed down the drain.

"I'm fine," I grumble.

"Vivian brought wine. Not the cheap kind, either," Carol says. "We poured you a glass."

I approach the coffee table and spot a giant glass of wine. The glass is not big, but the wine is touching the rim. I'm going to need to sip it without picking it up or I'll spill it. I kneel at the coffee table opposite the *Golden Girls* gang.

"I don't want to talk about it." I lean in and sip.

"We're just here to drink wine." Carol holds up her wineglass. "And hang out."

"That's what youths call it? Hanging out?" Vivian pinches the stem of her wineglass.

"I have no idea. I don't think I'm part of that crowd any-more." I sit and cross my legs, noticing a bowl of popcorn to my right that I didn't see when I first sat down. I grab a handful and shove the buttery kernels into my mouth.

"How was work?" Aunt Paula holds what looks like a glass of bubbly water.

Then I return to crying. I can't stop. I hear the ladies shifting on the couch and feel their hands on my shoulders, their whispers of *it's okay*. When I come up for air, I say, "I don't know how to be alone. I don't know what to do with my life."

"You can stay here and figure it out. We'll all help you," Carol says.

"Thank you, but I can't stay here. I must go home."

"Where is the home?" Rosa asks.

"I don't know." Then the tears turn into ugly, loud sobs.

# Chapter 26

I've had a few days to process Drew's visit, but I'm still crying a lot and unsure of how to move forward. So, I'm doing what I do best. Avoiding it. Which has allowed me to come up with a great plan, *not* for me, but for Herbert. To be fair, I'm giving myself credit for being able to think of anything other than anger and sadness.

"And you checked with your mom?" I whisper to Aaron as we sit in the shallow end of the pool. Aaron is in a vanilla donut inner tube, and I'm in one covered in a watermelon design. The sun has finally dipped behind the roof of Palms Place, and doing anything that doesn't involve my entire body underwater won't be happening. Ransom is also in a floaty, but it's more of a lounger. His front paws dangle off the side and his tail dips into the water as he rests his head on the pillowy area, looking sleepy.

"Yes, she said service animals are permitted," Aaron whispers and takes a sip of his beer encased in a cozy. "You really think that'll fix Herbert-Grumpy-Pants?"

"I think so." I dip lower into the water, allowing my chin to graze the surface, double-checking that no other residents are lurking. "I spotted a photo album with the name Gidget embossed on the spine with a paw print."

"Ahh, his anger comes from jealousy. Makes sense." He looks over at Ransom, then back at me. "What's the plan?"

"A few days ago, I assessed a woman who is needing placement in a nursing home. And she has the sweetest dog. I guess it was a service dog for her husband's PTSD, but he passed away six months ago. Unfortunately, the nursing home won't allow her to bring the dog. The good news is, she didn't seem too attached to it, which made me think about Herbert."

"You offered to take her late husband's dog?"

"It's better than taking it to the shelter. She loved the idea. And Aunt Paula told me about a study—crazy high numbers of illnesses about how horrible loneliness is for people of all ages, not just the elderly. Deep down, I think Herbert has a big heart."

"He's surrounded by people." Aaron motions around the courtyard at the apartments but keeps his voice to a whisper.

"Yes, he is, but you know how some married couples will say they feel alone, even though they live with a spouse?"

Aaron nods.

"Same thing. Aunt Paula said back when Herbert was in the Marines, he shared bunks with buddies, and after his service ended, he got married. He went from his family home into the military and then got married. Meaning he never lived alone."

"And what about you?"

"What about me?" I dip my head back into the water to wet my hair that is drying by the minute.

"What's the deal"—he puts his hand up, taking a swig of his beer—"with your soon-to-be ex?"

"I'm not going to fight him on the divorce."

"Welcome to the club."

My eyes widened. "Ugh. I need to figure out where I'll live. Not to mention how do I pack up my life? What is mine to take from our marriage? It's so overwhelming."

"I would start with your clothes. You should get all of those."

I snicker. "Yeah."

"And take the can opener. You'll never find a quality one these days." He nods his head and stares at his beer bottle.

"Speaking from experience, I take it."

He picks the edge of the label on his bottle. "I've been through three can openers in six months."

Ransom's floaty comes close enough to me that I reach out and pet his head. "I wish I could be as relaxed as you about life. Oh, to be a dog."

"I don't mind being a human. Opposable thumbs are rather handy."

"I think I'd give up my thumbs to live a dog's life." I tilt my head in his direction and Ransom lifts his head, sighs, and then lowers it as his eyes drift asleep.

"I think life is all about how you look at it." He uses his free hand and dips it into the water, making circles. "Yes, we make mistakes. I mean, criminals constantly claim they're wearing pants that don't belong to them."

I snuff a laugh through my nose.

"It's true. Every time we find something in their pockets, they're all, 'Man, these aren't my pants.' I've never met so many people wearing random pants."

I lean my head back and chuckle. "The things you've seen."

"Lots of unidentified pants." He smirks. "When my divorce was finalized, I realized I was the only one who could dig myself out of the hole. I still don't have the answers, and I might get married again, and divorced again, but it doesn't mean you stop trying."

"How can you be so optimistic? Once your mom comes back, you're without residency again."

"Trust me, I don't want to be living at Senior Citizens' Place forever."

"Oh, have you had Rosa's enchiladas?"

"I didn't have a choice. She showed up and had a yellow carnation on the top of the tinfoil. I think she was trying to win me over because she broke the garbage disposal right after I fixed the leaky sink. I ate that entire dish without Ransom's help. The next day, I was getting ready for my shift, and I could barely Velcro my vest on the side." He laughs, and I get warm fuzzies when I stare at him. "Can you move in with your aunt?"

"I can, temporarily, but I got a job offer this morning for a supervisory position back in Flag. I'd applied during a moment of frustration on an emotional day. And I promised my aunt I'd at least do the interview. I figured I could've gotten out of it since I'm down here, but they did it over Zoom."

"Congratulations?"

"Sort of. There are pluses and minuses, if I accept."

"Is going back to Flagstaff a plus or minus?"

"The position means a raise, so that would help me a-fford a place. Even though Drew and I are selling the house, we're in the red, so I don't expect any cash to help with a deposit or to cover first and last month's rent."

"Sounds like you have to take the position."

"Even with the raise, I'll need a roommate. And the position could be worse than what I'm currently doing. Somehow. Yes, my job is stressful. We don't have the re-sources we need. We deal with grumpy people. We're exposed to diseases and bugs. But what if the grass isn't greener on the other side?"

"Sometimes all the grass needs is a little water. And only you can water it."

I scrunch up my nose.

"Okay, what happens if you don't take the offer?"

"I'll stay in my current position and need *two* room-mates. To be honest, at my age, a roommate feels like going backwards in life. Plus, there are a lot of scary people out there."

"I can run a background check."

"That would be helpful, thank you." As I glance around, I can't help but feel more scared than ever. And it's not just about starting over all alone. The scariest part is the fear of making the same mistakes twice.

# CHAPTER 27

"Wait?" I clutch my work cell phone to my ear Friday evening right before I log off for the weekend. "What?"

"They're desperate down there for someone with experience, and they'll give you a raise to stay in Maricopa County, working mostly in the Sun City area. They also mentioned possibly training the newbies. I'll give you the weekend to think it over." My manager's words echo in my eardrums.

"Uh?" I feel as though I'm hallucinating.

"Enjoy your weekend. I'll speak with you on Monday."

The phone call ends. I'm frozen with my cell to my ear, gazing out my aunt's dining room window.

"What was that about?" Aunt Paula asks behind me as she mutes the TV.

"I thought I had everything somewhat figured out, but now I don't know what to do. Follow the safe path or take a new one? Either way, they're a risk."

"That's a good thing, right?"

"It means—" I pause. "I don't know what it means." I throw my hands up, go to the front door, and pull it open. The heat smacks me in the face. "And I can't even escape. I want to go for a walk, but it's like the devil owns the valley's thermostat."

I can feel I'm about to come unhinged. I'm over-whelmed. I'm scared. I'm worried. I need my parents. But I don't have them. I . . . I can't breathe and tears form.

"Calm down. Now come here and sit." Aunt Paula waves her hands at me when I spin around. "Stop all your crying."

She motions for me to sit on the floor in front of her re-cliner. I go on all fours and turn around, pushing my back into the recliner, wrapping my arms around my knees. Aunt Paula's fingers run through my hair like a brush. I'm reminded at that moment that my mom used to do this when I was little and needed calming down.

I'm not sure how many minutes pass, but I come out of my fog and hear my aunt's voice. I can't sit here and do nothing. But my brain won't stop spinning out of control. It's why meditation doesn't work for me. It makes everything worse. *Sit and clear your mind? Who can shut off their mind?* I'm not a magician. Meditation is for ma-gicians. I stand.

"Kelly, where are you going?"

"I'll be back." I grab my purse. "You need to eat. I'll tell Herbert on my way out. He can cook for you. I'm sorry." I swing open the door and again, without mercy, the heat smothers my face. "I'm sorry, I just can't sit around and think."

As soon as I shut the door, I notice the neon beehive that is Carol coming around to the left and Herbert to the right. Over the railing, in the pool, is George. Rosa is pushing Beverly in her wheelchair in the exterior's shade of the courtyard, and Beverly is shouting, "Go faster!" She's got her fall attire on—maple leaf sweatpants and matching T-shirt. Vivian is knocking on Aaron's door.

"Herbert, please help my aunt with dinner. I'll be back"—my hand goes out and wiggles—"sometime." I race down the steps and grab the rail, almost stumbling.

Herbert says something, but I don't hear what, his voice a mumble through the confusion in my head. Someone says hi and asks where I'm going, but I don't know who because I'm not paying attention. My focus is on the gate and beyond that, the parking lot. To my left, I spot Aaron and Ransom coming out of the apartment. I hear the door slam and Aaron mutters that he'll fix it later and storms past Vivian. We meet at the mailboxes and glare at each other for a second. It's apparent we're both on the same page. We walk ahead, and don't say a word to each other. We storm across the parking lot, and within a minute, we speed out of the complex, leaving a crisscross trail of rubber in our paths.

Both hands grip my aunt's Jeep steering wheel. Sweat forms under my palms as everything blurs on the road in front of me. I can't focus, which makes driving dangerous. Why does being an adult have to be complex? I don't know where I'm going, I'm just going. Back in Flag, I would go to Campbell Mesa Loop and wander the trails when I needed to get away. But here in Sun City, it seems like there is nowhere to escape. Especially since nearly every road is some giant freaking circle that loops you around the neighborhoods for eternity.

I make a turn here and there, and then another. I'm not paying attention to the road signs, and judging by a few honking horns, I'm not paying attention to much of anything. When I focus, I notice I've turned into Rio Vista Community Park, and I can't believe what I'm seeing. It's beautiful. There are long rows of trees shading the road as I ease the Jeep over the speed bumps, directing me into the center of the park. There are ponds and ducks wandering in the grass surrounding it. I pull into a spot and climb out. My heart is still racing along with my mind, but the massive trees and walking trails will at least allow me to feel less trapped in the cityscape. People are out, a lot of them, acting as though it's not hot.

I can't stop thinking about my choices, and I wish I didn't have any. Not having any choices would be better than having too many. And for me, two are too many. *Who let me become an adult?*

I follow the path towards the screams and squeals. Kids are running and jumping, smiles plastered across their faces. No cares, no worries, just freedom. They're playing on a splash pad while their parents look on from the benches under the cover of the awnings. I pause, watching them, and envy courses through me. I want to be free like that again. Free of decisions, choices, and what-ifs. My marriage failed. And I can't let my career fail, too.

I glance around, lost inside of myself. Lost in the right decision. And that's when I step forward, then I take another step, and another. Before I realize it, I'm right in the middle of the splash pad. Water is jetting up and kids in bathing suits and bare feet are running around me. I'm dressed in my clothes and shoes, but I don't care.

"What are you doing?" a child yells. "You have clothes on!"

"What are you doing?" I ask the child.

She shrugs her shoulders. "Having fun. But I have the right clothes on."

I glance down at my soaking wet T-shirt and shorts.

The child runs off, and I stand there, looking up at the parents and wondering what they think of me. I feel self-conscious about how this must look. How *I* must look. The crazy fully-dressed woman standing in the middle of a kids' splash pad. Then a mom rises from a bench and walks forward. She stomps her feet over one of the holes, causing the water to spray outward. She laughs, and a smile forms. We make eye contact, and she shouts over the kids, "We've been missing out, sitting on the sidelines."

"Indeed."

Then something happens. Several parents from the other benches kick off their shoes and invade on the kids' play space. The kids look shocked for a few seconds before they grab their parents' hands and run around with them. Maybe sometimes we all need to forget we're adults.

# Chapter 28

As I head through the gates of Palms Place, everyone is in the courtyard, and "She Works Hard for the Money" blasts from the speakers. The barbecue is smoking, and Carol fans the smoke as she flips a patty. I spot my aunt in the chair outside her apartment door. Ah, it's Friday.

"Kelly!" George cheers and raises his bottle of beer at me. "Just in time for chow!"

Vivian is at the closest table, pulling the lid off a container. "Why are you all wet?" She looks up at the sky as though she missed a storm.

"Splash pad," I shout over the music.

"You did that on purpose?" George points at me with his beer cozy.

"Change, you catch a cold," Rosa says without removing the cigarette from her mouth.

"In this oven, not possible." I move toward the exterior stairs.

"Hurry back," Carol calls over Donna Summer's voice. "No one likes a cold or burned burger."

I reach the landing and smile at my aunt as I round the banister.

"Have fun?" Aunt Paula points at me.

"I tried." I fling the keys around in my hand.

I ease into the empty chair next to Aunt Paula. Together, we watch the scene below. I realize how much it feels like home here. It's only been a few weeks, but Palms Place really is unique in the best of ways. Who would have thought hanging out with a bunch of senior citizens would bring me peace and joy?

"I'm glad you found this apartment complex." I reach over and squeeze her hand.

"Me too."

Vivian comes up the stairs. "Did you tell her yet?"

I look at my aunt and then back at Vivian. "Tell me what?"

"Shh, Viv. She's sopping wet and probably hungry. It can wait."

"What can wait?"

"We don't even know what she's decided. And I don't want to sway her decision." Aunt Paula crosses her arms.

"*Bien, peu importe*," Vivian huffs. "Hurry, go change, it's time to eat."

I'm not sure what's going on, so I walk backwards to the front door and ease it open, keeping my eyes on the two women until the very last second.

My aunt insists I eat with the rest of the residents down by the pool, but I want to spend time with her. I balance the plate of chips and hamburger on the top of my knees as I stare out into the courtyard below. Aunt Paula has her meal on a TV tray as her feet soak in the kiddie pool underneath it.

"Want to talk about it?" Aunt Paula brings the hot dog to her mouth.

"Pros and cons list is equally balanced." I take a bite of burger, catching the melted cheese as it oozes out the bottom with my pinkie. "*Was* balanced. I got to thinking when I was standing on the splash pad. Sometimes change isn't for the better. Maybe I needed to change how I look at something versus change what I look at."

My aunt nods her head. "And what does that mean for you?"

"I want to spend more time with you. I want to live my life. Maybe I've struggled with my job because deep down inside, I'm searching for perfection. Perfection from my job, my marriage, and from myself. But that's not life; and starting over is scary. Sort of like the dark. And I feel if I learn to understand it, then maybe it won't be scary." I feel like Kevin in *Home Alone* when he overcomes the basement. "Allowing my job to make me unhappy and to bleed over into my personal life is unfair. It's a part of me, but not the whole me. This"—I gesture out to the courtyard below—"is what I need to work on. My life outside of work. And that, I hope, will help with any job I have. I just need to figure out what I should do, take the new job in Flag, or go for the raise here."

"Well, maybe I can help with that."

I pick up my glass of iced tea from the ground next to my feet. "How so?"

"Vivian and I got to talking about my house."

"Your house? I hate to break it to you, Aunt Paula, but I'm not fifty-five, and I can't afford to buy it."

"Why does that matter?" She sets her cheese-less burger on the plate. "What if I don't sell my house?"

"And you would move back there?"

"No, it's time to make new memories, here, at Palms Place. Besides, Herbert is a lot of fun to live next door to. He's growing on me."

"Aunt Paula!" I smack the side of her arm. "While I appreciate the offer, that house is too big for just one person. And by law, in Sun City at least one person in the home must be fifty-five or older."

"It's in Youngtown."

"What?" I blink.

"When was the last time you mailed me a card?"

"My mom always mailed them when I was little, and when I got older, I guess I always called. But Mom always said, 'Let's go to your aunt's in Sun City.'" I shake my burger at her. "And the navigation in the car says . . . wait, I know my way here. So, I never use it."

"Exactly, and that drove me nuts that she never could remember. My house address is Youngtown. Palms Place is Sun City."

I sigh. "Regardless, I can't cover the mortgage on a place that big."

"You can't, and I can't offer any discounts because I'm living on social security and a small pension."

"Thank you, anyway. It was a nice offer."

Aunt Paula reaches out for my arm. "Let me finish. You can do it with a roommate."

"Yes, yes, I could do that." Then I think about having to find a decent person to share my space with, even though Aaron would run a background check for me.

"With Aaron."

I lean over my plate as my head turns toward her. "I think maybe I have water in my ears. Did you say Aaron?"

She nods her head and bites another bit of her hot dog. Her mouth is too full to answer, and I feel as though this is on purpose.

"Aaron is a boy. I mean a man. Have you not seen *When Harry Met Sally*?"

"What's with all the Meg Ryan movie references around here?" She takes a sip of her drink. "We can trust Aaron. Plus, we know where his mom lives if he doesn't behave."

"And you asked him?"

"I did, after Vivian directed him, against his will, to see me."

Just then, everyone down by the pool cheers, "Aaron!"

I stand and move to the railing. Aaron and Ransom approach the first table closest to his mom's apartment. I can't see his face from up there, but his posture is firm, his arm rigid, holding Ransom's leash.

George says something to him, but I can't hear what.

"No, I don't want your burgers or hot dogs." Aaron's voice is loud and carries up to the terrace. "Now, shut everything down. It's too loud."

Herbert shuts off the music and the complex falls silent. I can hear the traffic on the road behind us. Then Aaron and Ransom enter his mom's apartment, and the door slams closed.

I step back and ease into the chair. "So, you want me to room with Officer Grumpy Pants?"

My aunt raises an eyebrow. "Vivian and I refer to him as Officer Grouchy."

# CHAPTER 29

When I wake in the morning, I stare up at the popcorn ceiling in my aunt's bedroom. Did I dream the barbecue, splash pad, and my aunt wanting me to rent her house with Aaron? I bring my hand to my face and rub my right eye. I shake my head. "Must've been a dream."

I throw back the sheets and head out of the bedroom into the living room.

"Good morning, sunshine," Aunt Paula says from her recliner.

"Morning." I flop onto the couch. "I had the most realistic dream."

"What was it about?"

"Wait, it wasn't a dream." I move to the edge of the couch. "Did you suggest I rent your house with Aaron?"

"Yes, I did."

"Do you call him Officer Grouchy?"

"Correct again." She smiles.

I let out a breath. "It wasn't a dream."

"I suggest you get dressed. I was part of the group text, and you've been nominated to go talk to Aaron."

"What?" I lean forward and my hand goes to the coffee table to brace myself from falling into it.

"When there's an issue, we group text."

"Palms Place group texts?"

"Are you sure you're fine? You're repeating an awful lot."

I huff and smack my hand to my forehead. "And you all voted that I talk to Aaron first thing in the morning?"

Aunt Paula checks her watch on her wrist. "It's nine thirty. That's not early."

I place both hands on either side of my thighs and push myself up to stand. "And that is why I'm not living here. You're all crazy."

I make my way to the door and fling it open.

"Kel, you're in your pajamas."

I glance down and turn back to look at her. "Yes, maybe it'll be more welcoming when I knock on his door"—I air quote—"*this* early in the morning."

My bare feet pad down the stairs and across the courtyard, the concrete already warm. Normally, at least one of the residents is out and about, but it's a ghost town and it appears as though FNF never occurred last night.

I swallow and make a fist, gently rapping on the door to apartment 1. Nothing. I decide to knock again, a little harder this time. Nothing. I pivot to leave when I hear the door open behind me. I turn to find Aaron, his hair going in all directions, and a scruffy shadow on his jawline.

"What's broken?" He looks me up and down. "Why are you walking around in your pajamas?"

"I'm not walking around, I came to talk to you. And I'm not in the mood to get dressed. It's too early." I push past him as though he's invited me.

"Sure, come on in."

Ransom hurries over, his stuffed alligator clutched in his mouth, and sits up against my right leg. He puts enough pressure on me that I have to brace myself so I don't fall over. "I don't know what happened last night, but you were very rude to everyone." I point my finger at Aaron and then poke his chest. "What is up with you?"

He blinks. "You've got a lot of nerve poking me, let alone this early, let alone on a weekend, let alone in pajamas with teddy bears on them."

"Do not insult my teddy bears." I cross my arms, realizing I don't have a bra on. I really need to remember this before I storm out of places.

Ransom noses me in the hip, and when I glance down, his eyes seem to smile while he clutches his alligator in his mouth.

"Sorry," Aaron whines and shakes his head. "Last night was horrific. A traffic stop went bad. The officer is in the hospital."

I reach out and set my hand on the side of his tricep. "I'm sorry. Will the officer make it?"

"The doctors say she'll be okay." Aaron runs his hand through his hair.

"That's good." I set my on hand on Ransom's head, stroking his soft fur.

"Are you hungry? I can make us breakfast. I figure we should talk about the roommate thing."

"Ah yes, Aunt Paula and Vivian spoke with you. Do you think it'll work?" I follow him to the edge of the kitchen and Ransom tags along.

"I don't know. I mean, from what I got from your aunt, the house seems like it's plenty big for us to keep out of each other's hair. And if my girls ever wanted to come and spend time with me, there would be a room for them."

He holds up a carton of eggs, and I nod my head. "That's a bonus."

"I didn't want to seem too eager, but it's been a challenge for me to find someplace I can afford that allows

Ransom and is in a decent neighborhood." Aaron cracks eggs against the side of the pan on the stove. "But I thought you didn't know if you were taking the promotion in Flagstaff."

"I thought so, too. At least that was what I was leaning towards, but I got an offer to stay here, and it involves a raise. And while I love it up there, the possibility of running into Drew or his extended family is not something I'm looking forward to."

"You're close with his family?"

"Not at all, and now it's a blessing." I ease onto a barstool at his mom's kitchen peninsula and watch him whisk the eggs into a scramble. Ransom hops onto the couch and flops down. "Do you see your ex a lot?"

"More than I'd like, and usually with her new husband." He pushes the eggs around as they cook. "So, you're going to stay in your current position?"

I lean my elbows on the peninsula. "I think so. A part of me worries it means I'm not growing or wanting more of myself career-wise by not taking the management position."

He looks up at me, then back to the stove. "I say do what you want to do. I think society measures success only as moving up." Aaron holds up a blue coffee mug from the cupboard. "Maybe sometimes moving sideways is better."

"Coffee would be great. But you lost me on moving sideways."

He sticks a pod into the machine and pushes the handle. "Are we any less to the world without fancy job titles like lawyer or astronaut?"

"That's true."

"Working hard and showing dedication is underrated these days. Look at farmers and truck drivers. Without them, we don't eat. We should focus on the good we do and forget about achieving some fancy label." He winks, and my heart skips.

I lean further forward as he slides a mug of coffee my way, steam coming from it. He sets French vanilla and cinnamon bun coffee creamer in front of me. "I may not have a fancy title, but you do."

"I do?"

"My aunt and Vivian call you Officer Grouchy. I call you Officer Grumpy Pants."

He laughs and I'm reminded it's such a great laugh. "That's almost as good as your nickname."

"What?" I squawk.

"Oh, you didn't know? Everyone around here calls you Kelly Cat."

I lean back on the stool and lift the mug to my lips. "Why?"

"Because they say you're as adorable as a cat but also feisty."

I hold my mug out, and he picks up his. "Well, then Officer Grumpy Pants, are you ready to be my roommate?"

"I sure am, Kelly Cat."

# Chapter 30

With all the new things on my plate, I forgot about picking up Herbert's surprise. Thankfully, my client was very understanding, and she had yet to move into assisted living. I think she was happy to spend an extra day with the dog.

I park my aunt's Jeep in her spot. As I climb out, I long for my Nissan. Hopefully, it'll only be in the shop for another week.

"Alright, fella." I pop open the passenger door. "Are you ready to surprise Herbert?" The four-year-old black-and-white Lab-pointer mix tilts his head, and his right ear flops over as though he's still a puppy.

I text Aaron I'm here. The pavement is far too hot, and I can't manage carrying a sixty-pound dog all the way up to Herbert's apartment. I was already going to be sore tomorrow from carrying him twenty feet from his prior home to the Jeep.

Aaron comes up behind me. "Okay, maybe we don't tell Herbert about this one and we just take it with us to your aunt's house." He leans around me and rubs both sides of the dog's ears. The dog's eyes roll back in delight. "He's freaking adorable."

"We're not even roommates yet and already talking about kids," I joke as Aaron hoists the dog out of the passenger seat.

"It's best to be prepared. We could end up with a ton of dogs." He grins. "How was work?"

I follow him as we walk through the gate, amazed at how quickly we seem to have become friends. "No bedbugs today, and no one yelled at me. So, pretty good."

We peek around the bank of mailboxes into the courtyard.

"Okay, all clear." I wave him to move forward.

We make our way up the stairs and take the long way around, so we don't have to pass directly in front of Herbert's apartment. I slide the key into my aunt's apartment door, and all three of us slip in as quietly as can be.

"Oh, gosh, he's a cutie." Aunt Paula leans forward in her recliner. "Herbert's going to fall in love."

"Okay, Aunt Paula, showtime," I say.

She picks up her cell phone and scrolls left and right, and then holds the phone to her ear. "Herbert, would you mind coming over? I have a minor problem, and I hope you can help me with it." She nods and ends the call. "Okay, he's coming."

Aaron and I are standing with the dog between us as Herbert knocks on the door.

"Come in," Aunt Paula calls out.

Herbert opens the door and steps inside. "Is everything alright, Ms. Paula?" Then he looks at us and spots the dog. "Is *this* the problem?" His hands go up in the air. "Well, of course, a dog. Another dog." His hands move to his hips. "Don't you think one dog is enough, Mr. Aaron?"

"I do." Aaron holds out the leash. "And that is why you should have this one."

Herbert freezes, and I see him swallow as his Adam's apple shifts. "What? I can't. What?" His voice shakes. "Me?"

I step forward and take the leash from Aaron. The Lab pointer follows. "This is Nick. He's a service dog. His owner passed, and the wife can't keep him."

"But." Herbert takes the leash, and I swear it looks like he's about to cry.

I set my hand on his shoulder. "No buts, Herbert. He's a service dog, which means he's allowed to be here at Palms Place. Don't worry, we double-checked with Marie, you know, rules and all."

Herbert kneels and wraps his hands on the dog's shoulders. "He's mine? Nick is mine?"

"He's all yours." I smile.

"But I've been so mean about Ransom and Ms. Rosa and her contraband dog." Herbert remains kneeling, petting the dog's head over and over.

"Yes, Herbert," Aunt Paula says. "You've been a real butthead at times."

"But," Aaron emphasizes, "we know it was only because of your love for animals and how unfair it felt to you."

"I don't deserve him." Herbert gives the dog a hug.

"We all deserve good things." I glance back at Aaron.

"Ms. Kelly, Mr. Aaron, I don't know what to say." Herbert stands and keeps his grip around the leash as though the dog might run off.

"How about a nice dinner, the dogs and us?" I smile.

"Only if I can cook it, Ms. Kelly."

"Oh, I expect it." I laugh and give him a hug.

"Ms. Kelly, you're right, about change being scary. But if you're surrounded by love and supported with goodness, then it might be a little easier."

And he's right. I might not be sure about my choices regarding my pending divorce, my pending move, my pending roommate, or my increased responsibilities at work. But I know I can always make a change if I don't like the outcome. Because living life isn't about accepting or ignoring change, it's about your attitude towards the change.

# The End

# Aunt Paula's Edible Cookie Dough

2 tbsp room temperature salted butter

2 tbsp white sugar

2 tbsp brown sugar

- 1 tbsp sour cream

- ¼ tsp vanilla extract

- 4 tbsp white flour

- ¼ tsp baking soda

- 3 tbsp of your favorite chocolate chips

Hand mix all ingredients until smooth and creamy. Enjoy or place in the refrigerator until more chilled to your liking.

# ACKNOWLEDGEMENTS

To my family and friends who have joined me on my writing journey, thank you.

Of course, I couldn't do it without you, the reader, THANK YOU!!

Thank you, Krista, my editor who has been with me for many books over the years.

My PAWS Readers (much love to you all!) who are always so eager for my next book. You make me so happy when I hit send and you dive right in!

A big thanks to my author friends that show me so much support.

A special thanks to Janet Porter, Sandy Herzog, and Linda Martin for being BIG fans!

# ABOUT THE AUTHOR

Annually, 10% of the proceeds from the sale of this book, and all Savannah's books are donated to dog rescue organizations ~ READING IS BETTER WITH A DOG

Savannah Hendricks (born in California, raised in Washington, and resides in Arizona) is a full-time social worker and fills as much of her weekends as possible with writing. She loves all things dog-related, has a passion for red wine, gardening, baking, and creating yummy recipes. You'll often find her hollering at the TV during restoration shows when they paint over red bricks.

If you'd love a digital personalized autograph or bookplate, you can request one by visiting: savannahhendrick s.com

Please discover more about Savannah by interacting with her on:

Instagram: savannahhendricks_author

Facebook: AuthorSavannahHendricks

# ALSO BY SAVANNAH

Heartfelt Coming of Age/Women's Fiction
***Sun City, 85373***
***The Album*** (Multi-Award-Winning)
***I Adopted My Mom at the Bus Station*** (Multi-Award-Winning)

Humorously Wholesome Romance
***Route to Romance***
***A Hearts of Woolsey series: A Desert Restoration, A Desert Romance, A Desert Rivalry***
***The Christmas Rental***
***Grounded in January*** (Award-Winning)
***Grounded in July***
***To Work Out or to Wed***

<u>Meaningful Picture Books</u>
*Where Does "I Love You" Go?*
*The Needle-less Christmas Tree & Other Tree Tales*
*Winston Versus the Snow* (Multi-Award-Winning)
*Nonnie and I* (Available in English, Spanish & Bilingual)